# THE LONELY GIRL

## MARCUS BLAKE

~ THE MARCUS BLAKE COLLECTION ~

# The Lonely Girl

A Mavericknes Media / Truesource Publishing  book



The Lonely Girl  was edited by
Carol Felder and J M Almgreen

The story is fictional and any resemblance to actual
people, places, and certain facts associated with the
characters created by Marcus Blake is purely
coincidence.

Mavericknes Media : Dallas Texas

Truesource Publishing : Dallas Texas

www.truesourcepublishing.com

ISBN : 978-1-932996-56-2

Printed in the United States of America
Published in Dallas, Texas

For More information on Marcus Blake go to....

www.marcusblake.net
www.facebook.com/themarcusblake
www.twitter.com/marcusblake
www.thatnerdshow.com

# ABOUT THE AUTHOR

Marcus Blake was born in Chicago, Illinois in 1977. He grew up in Chicago and East Texas. His education is in History, Literature, Psychology, and Religion & Philosophy. Marcus Blake has studied at many universities throughout the United States, but his Alma Mater is Stephen F. Austin State University in Nacogdoches, Texas, which is also where he wrote his first book, The Music of Life. Marcus Blake is a Poet, Musician, Comedian, Writer, and Historian. His books are The Music of Life, My Reflections, Returning Home. Sex Game. The Lonely Girl, Stories From Wrigley, 30 Minutes: Trust and Lies, 30 Minutes: Guilty Until Proven Innocent, 30 Minutes: A Soldier's Song, and 30 Minutes: A Badge of Honor. . He has taught in the public school system, served in the Army, and been a guest speaker at Education and Literary events throughout the world. Marcus Blake is also a Radio Host, his current show is Saturday Morning Nerd Show which can be heard on Saturday Mornings at www.thatnerdshow.com. He is a veteran of Rock and Roll shows as well as Political shows on the radio. Marcus Blake makes his home in the Dallas, Texas.

Other Books by Marcus Blake...

*The Music of Life*

*My Reflections*

*Sex Game*

*Returning Home*

*Stories From Wrigley*

*30 Minutes: Trust and Lies*

*30 Minutes: Guilty Until Proven Innocent*

*30 Minutes: A Soldier's Song*

*30 Minutes: A Badge of Honor*

*Ring of Warriors: Making a Fighter*

This book is dedicated to someone that I once loved. Thank you for showing me a dark world that I never knew and also for showing me what was possible within myself. I will always be a better person for having known you. My hope is that one day you find what you're looking for even if I am not meant to travel the same road with you.

"My friend...care for your psyche...know thyself, for once we know ourselves, we may learn how to care for ourselves"

– *Socrates*

# Prologue

**R**ome was burning, she thought to herself – at least that's the way it seemed for Lisa. Her life was in shambles. She had always said that her great life was like Rome at the height of its power, she was also fond of saying "when in Rome do like the Romans do." Everything in her life that had once been great had now turned to shit. She wasn't mad about that as she sat on the bench at the police station, handcuffed, waiting to be processed. She was mad that she couldn't figure out why especially since she was good at figuring out puzzles. She was educated, she was beautiful, she was successful in her career, and she wasn't a junkie or an alcoholic. There was no explanation for any of this, no reason she shouldn't be happy, but here she was at the police station handcuffed to a bench.

Lisa was arrested a couples of hours before for yelling at a convenience store clerk and provoking him with racial slurs. She was trying to get a rise out of him and one eye witness even said that she had used the term "Arab Nigger," while acting like she was going to steal something. She was hoping that the clerk would take the bait and shoot her. After all it was a bad part of the city where people were known to be trigger happy. Here dramatics did get a reaction- the police were called and she was arrested for disturbing the peace. As she sat on the bench Lisa was thinking about that, she was thinking "why doesn't someone just fucking kill me and get it over with."

The police officers who brought her in were on the other side of the room talking to their captain. Lisa could see them, but she didn't know what they were saying, she couldn't even read their lips even though she knew how. They had their backs turned to her.

"What do we do with her?" the female officer asked the captain.

"Well, what's her story? She wasn't breaking any laws, just causing a nuisance in the store. Hell, she didn't even resist arrest. We really have nothing to hold her on," the captain replied.

Before the female officer could reply her partner Officer Benton spoke up. "We ran her through the system and while she doesn't have any priors except for a few traffic violations – she did go the hospital a couple of times over the last ten years and both times she had to talk to a police officer."

The captain asked Benton. "So why did she have to talk to the police."

"It seems that both cases were suicide attempts- one instance she took too many pills and the other she ran a red light plowing into a city bus. Both times in her statement she said that it was just an accident even though witnesses said something different"

"Well she isn't very original in her excuses. It also sounds like that staying alive isn't a priority for her."

The female officer replied. "There's something else though. Both times she was diagnosed as depressed and suicidal by a hospital shrink and given high doses of medication, then ordered to go to counseling."

"Let me guess she ignored that advice, took the drugs and never followed up with the shrink."

"That's true, and shrinks had almost the same exact reports." The female officer replied. "There were also reports of anger issues, violent outbursts, and encouragement towards other people to harm her. And when we arrested her she had been carrying a knife in her purse and took it out slamming it on the counter while she dug around in her purse. And then she proceeded to throw change at him while at the same time calling the clerk racial names."

The Captain sighed and thought for a moment. Then he replied "Okay so we have the same MO here. You think she's suicidal and trying to get someone to kill her so she doesn't have to do it herself."

"That's exactly what I think she's doing. This woman doesn't need a jail cell, she needs a shrink." the female officer replied.

"Okay then, book her and send her over to the county psych ward to get evaluated. Make sure you put in the report everything you told me so we can keep her for 10 days while the County Psychologist can check her out."

The police officers got Lisa up off the bench, uncuffed her and walked her to a desk then sat her down. They got out all the paperwork and proceeded to fill out the long reports starting with information from her state ID

Lisa asked the female officer who was taking the report. "How do you know that all that information is correct?"

"Are you telling me that's it not?" the female officer replied."

"Now why would I lie to you?"

"You lied to us about what you really were doing at that store."

"I did not."

"You did to and besides you weren't robbing the place so there's no reason to hide your identity or where you live."

"True so I am not lying about anything."

"Oh you're lying to us, just not about who you are."

Lisa looked away so she didn't have to look the female officer in the eye. After a pause she asked the officer. "What would I be lying about?"

The female officer forced Lisa to look at her then she replied. "You're lying about the fact that you wanted the clerk to kill you – you're suicidal."

Lisa was shocked at the statement, but she didn't deny it either. She didn't say anything else to the officer. She looked away in anger while the female officer finished the paperwork. After that was done

Lisa finally asked, "so what now, you putting me in jail?"

"No you're going to county Mental facility for 10 days to be evaluated. If you get to be set free it'll be a doctor who decides."

"How dare you, you fucking bitch."

The female officer just stared at her and then smiled. "Call me anything you want, but you're still going and our report will still say that you're suicidal."

Lisa gave her a dirty look and then asked her. "What about my phone call, I at least get a phone call."

"You'll get one once you get to the hospital."

"This is bullshit; I still get a phone call."

"Who would you call?"

"What."

"Who would you call – you don't have someone to call do you."

Lisa was shocked again at the officer's statement to her. She didn't know what to really say, but she managed anyway.  She replied back. "You don't know that – you don't know anything about me."

The female officer looked at her and said. "I do you know you. You're a poor lonely girl looking for attention, but this time it's in the form of suicide, although I'm sure no one will care if you do it or not.

You're all alone because you've probably pushed everyone out of your life that ever really meant anything."

"You're still wrong. All you're doing is judging me."

"Believe what you want to believe, but if you really wanted a phone call and needed to call someone then that would have been the first thing you asked for when we brought you in."

Lisa was silent. She knew it was going to be a long ten days and she also knew that Officer Reyes was right. She didn't have anyone, she was all alone. The only untrue part in the police officer's comment was that she had pushed everybody away – she never did that, they had all left her. Lisa was the victim and that's what she had been telling herself all these years.

∞ ∞ ∞ ∞ ∞

The room Lisa was in at the hospital was filled with dirty white walls and they looked like they hadn't been cleaned in a years. They had the look of abandonment – nobody cared about the walls so nobly bothered to clean them. That was all Lisa could think as she stared at the dirty white walls while waiting to be processed in the hospital. She had been waiting in the check in room for about an hour since she arrived and nobody had spoken to her. Nobody cared about her, she was just one more patient, one more lunatic looking for the good drugs and an excuse to not have to live in the real world. That was the stereotype of most patients that came into the hospital and the truth was she did fit the bill, but she had her own unique story of how she ended up there.

Finally a nurse began to check her in. They took her information down and copied down what was in the police report. The things that she had on her at the time of her arrest were searched again for weapons or drugs. Then she was taken into a room and strip searched. It was humiliating and again no one cared how she felt. She was just a crazy patient looking for the good drugs –she was accused of that from the staff and the police officer's who brought her in on more than one occasion. Lisa was starting to believe it. She dressed in her white hospital gown and then given some cheap thin soled slippers to wear.  Finally she was done checking in.

She was led down a long narrow hallway to sounds of crazy rants and horrifying screams. As she was lead down the hallway out of the corner of her eye she could see the windows in the individual rooms and they were covered with bars. For the first time since arriving she knew she was in a prison. As it turned out, it was her own prison, but that will be explained later because it was lights out on the ward. They found a bed for her and made her get into it – she was restrained as per the orders of the police when she arrived. After all she was a suicide victim and the only thing the hospital cared about was that she didn't kill herself in her sleep.

After she was restrained her roommate in the next bed whispered to her. "Hey girly when the visitors from Tridian 54 come for me tonight, I will make sure they do not take your brain. It's your first night here and you might need it." Her roommate, who was also named Lisa, but preferred to be called *Lisa of Earth,* just wanted to warn her – it was an introduction to the nuthouse.  She just simply smiled at Lisa before she turned over in her bed facing the opposite wall and began to cry. Lisa couldn't help but feel afraid and she too shed a few tears. She began to cry and it was the most real thing she had done in a very long time. It was the sanest thing she had done tonight.

# DAY 1

It was day one in the hospital for Lisa and she was still feeling just as shitty as she had felt the night before. She was also more scared than the night before because she was getting her first real glimpse of the place.  About an hour after breakfast Lisa finally met with the doctor. She was led into an office that had the same dirty white walls as the rest of the ward, but there was a difference, there were a few pictures hanging on the wall. They were the same kind of pictures that you would fine in a counselors office or a school classroom – motivational pictures that said things like *live for your dreams* and *the only chances you miss are the ones you don't take*. The office was a cliché and not very comforting.

The doctor was sitting in a chair reading through a file and so the orderlies made Lisa sit down in the chair opposite of the doctor and wait. Since Lisa's arrival at the hospital she was always being made to wait for something. It seemed as if it was some kind of test to see how long it would take before she got irritated, at least that's all Lisa could think of. Lisa looked around the room and then at the doctor – the doctor hadn't once looked at her since entering the room. After about 5 minutes of just sting there and waiting the doctor finally spoke, but didn't look at her while doing it, she continued to stare at the file.

The doctor asked Lisa. "So it looks like you want to kill yourself?"

"What, I never said that, in fact I've been telling everybody since I was arrested that I'm not suicidal."

"According to this report, you tried to get a clerk at a gas station to shoot you by calling him an Arab Nigger."

"I might have called him that, but that doesn't mean I want to kill myself. I was mad at the guy."

"Well you did call him that and then you slammed a butcher knife from your purse on the table while taunting him according to eye witnesses. There would be no reason to do that if you didn't want him to react and I think you knew he would reach for the gun behind the counter."

"What's your point doctor?"

"How are you not at least a little suicidal if you're trying to get someone else to kill you?"

Lisa didn't say anything. She just looked away so she didn't have to see the doctor staring at her. There was a pause in the conversation for about 30 seconds and all that time Lisa looked away staring at the dirty white walls. The doctor finally spoke again. "It's okay Lisa, you don't have to answer the question- your body language has already given me your answer. I just want to point out that you're not fooling anybody around her."

Lisa gave the doctor a sharp look and replied. "I don't care what you're report says, you don't know what you're talking about."

"So you're here for other reasons? Are you trying to score some good drugs?"

"You know you're about the fourth person to suggest that since I got here, what's the deal with the accusation?"

The doctor smiled at her as she looked up from the file and her notepad. Then she said. "You seem aware and that's good. We have three types of patients here – the mentally ill, who will need constant care for the rest of their lives, we have those that are looking for an escape – a bed for a few days while trying to score some really powerful drugs so they'll say anything to get what they want. Then we have those that are not mentally ill, they need someone to help them see the truth in their problems because they usually can't face the truth about themselves.  Attempted suicides are a good way to find the help they need."

Lisa looked at the doctor with a stern look and asked her. "So which one am I...you must have it figured it out already."

"I have an idea, but we're going to be talking even more so I can come up with a definite answer. "

"What if I don't want to talk?"

"Then you will be here a lot longer than ten days. Do you want to stay any longer?"

"No, I don't, but I don't want to talk to you either."

"I will mark this down as your first truthful answer since arriving here, but also keep in mind that you don't get it both ways. You want to leave then you have to talk to me and we can talk about anything you want to in your life as along as we get to the truth about why you're really here."

Lisa sighed. She was mad, but she knew that she the doctor was right; she couldn't have it both ways. We rarely ever get it both ways.

The doctor let her know that the first session was done and that she would be back to talk to her in the afternoon. She gathered her things and the orderlies came in to get Lisa and escort her back to her room. As she walking out the doctor looked at her and said. "By the way, I have a rule, once you give me your first truthful answer; I introduce myself so we can talk like regular people. May name is Dr. Emily Bennett. Truth around here gets you respect and civility."

Lisa looked at her and replied. "Thank you, my name is Lisa, nice to meet you."

Dr. Bennett smiled and replied. "That is your second truthful answer. You're doing well so far."

∞ ∞ ∞ ∞ ∞

The clock was ticking. The gap was widening. Lisa's own reality was becoming a blur from what she thought to be true and the drug intoxicated dream she was having while in the hospital. She sat there at the table in the cafeteria playing with her stale mash potatoes trying to figure out how she got into the mental facility. She didn't have an answer. Lisa didn't even really want to talk about anything that could make her find the answer. She had convinced herself a long time ago that not knowing was always better.  Lisa also liked to say that ignorance was bliss.

After a while a fellow patient sat down next to her. It was another woman, older and more cynical, her ideas defined by the years she had spent at this hospital. She had been sentenced here after she killed her husband and then tried to kill herself. At least that's what Lisa chose to believe – Lisa always had a gift for fiction. The patient seemed happy, but perhaps it was just sarcasm. Her tone was different than the other patients and it made Lisa take notice. The woman introduced herself as Rose.

"So you're the new patient?" Rose said.

"I guess I am."

"How do you like it so far?"

"I have never been to a place like this before so I have nothing to compare it to."

"Well I've been to three different hospitals and this one is by far the best. It's easier to deal with, easier to escape from everything, and it's definitely better because no one cares." Rose then gave off this hideous laugh that would make even a hyena run away. Lisa didn't know if it was on purpose or she just laughed that way, but it was frightening in a way and perhaps that was the purpose. Lisa was creeped out now and didn't want to talk to Rose, but

Rose wouldn't just let her out of the conversation that easily.

"Don't be afraid my dear. There are worst things to be afraid of."

"Oh, like what?"

"Other patients, there's one named Bud who likes to pee on people."

Lisa gave her a strange look, she had never heard of something like that before, but she was in a Psych Ward, strange behavior was normal in a place like this. Rose smiled at her, trying not to be too weird, but with as much medication as she was on there was no way to control how she acted. She couldn't keep still and she was mumbling to herself when she wasn't talking to Lisa.

So Lisa finally asked. "Is this what I have to look forward to when I'm on medication?"

"If you assume that you're not ever leaving here."

"Well I'm leaving in ten days."

"Maybe, maybe not."

"I am leaving in ten days."

"That's what most people think when they arrive, but they don't. They make a new home here, isolated from everything they hold dear."

Lisa gave a puzzled look at Rose because her tone and her words were familiar, like she had heard them before. It was as if the voice was her very own, at least that's the way it seemed. Lisa didn't know why she felt the familiarity in the conversation, but she did. It was freaky in a way, something like dejavu. Lisa asked Rose.

"So why are you here?"

"They put me here."

"Who put you here?"

"The ones I loved."

Lisa paused for a moment, watching Rose and her systematic actions. Her actions were like a ritual, they had a rhythm and it was fascinating to watch, Lisa had to admit. She also knew that's what happened when you were in place like this – all your actions are weird to outsiders, but rhythmic and comforting to you. She was also nervous watching Rose because she could see herself like that in about ten years from now. And so she had to ask the expert of a place like this.

"Rose do you think I'm going to be here after ten days."

"It's not up to me…it's up to you, but you've already made your decision."

"What…why do you say that?"

"Because it's easy to be here."

Lisa gave her a surprised look. She didn't know how to respond to that, but she was going to try the question anyway. As she started to say something Rose grabbed her arms and pulled herself closer to Lisa, she was face to face with her. She said to her in a serious tone.

"Being here is easy – it's easier to walk through those doors than to leave. You're safe here and the bars on the windows keep you locked away and safe from the ugly world that's too damn hard to deal with.  You would rather be here than out there or you would just get up and walk out right now, but you don't."

Rose smiled at her either to let her know that everything was okay or just to make Lisa feel more weird – there was no telling what Roses' real intentions were. Then she said one final thing before scampering off to bother someone else. "Decisions were already made – you'll stay and if you don't want to then you wouldn't have ended up here in the first place." After that Rose was gone and Lisa was a little shook up. It was hard to tell whether she was just talking gibberish, but truth has a funny way of showing itself sometimes.

Lisa just wanted to go back to her room now and so she did. She crawled into bed and curled up trying to ignore everything around her including her roommate who was talking in some kind of weird language. Her roommate called it the alien language. Lisa began to cry again, and she just cried herself to sleep until her next session with the doctor.

∞ ∞ ∞ ∞ ∞

Lisa slept for about two hours and while asleep she traveled in her dreams. She dreamed about her mother, something she hadn't done in a long time. Lisa wasn't that fond of her mother, too many bad memories and it was better to forget. That's what she had told herself all these years.

Her mother had been the worst kind. She was naïve and overbearing; she couldn't make a good decision to save her life, and having children thrown into the mix just made it worse. When she dreamed of her mother it was always the same dream. The one was where her mother had thrown her out of the house and for the most part, told her that she didn't love her anymore. It was always so vivid and it was so etched into her mind that she could remember every minute of it, every second of it because it was the beginning of the end for her.

So there she was in her room again not too long after getting home from school and her mother was already drunk. They were living somewhere in Texas now after mom had gotten married for the third time. This time to some truck driver from the east coast who was hardly ever around. Lisa couldn't recall how they really hooked up but it was probably the same old story knowing her mother – she hooked up with a guy who bought her a few drinks and then somehow convinced herself that she loved him. Lisa knew better and after her mother would sober up she would see the hard truth as well. That's what Lisa was hoping for, but it was wishful thinking on her part.

Her mother was notorious for finding someone with money and she was also good at convincing herself that she did it for her children. This last marriage was more convenient than anything else – she needed a place to stay, a husband that made good money to support her kids and her drinking habits, and the guy just needed a fuck buddy when he got home from the road. He was a truck driver so it was perfect. They didn't have to see each other, he didn't have to be a parent, and when he did get home they would get loaded and fuck for days. It was a match made in heaven.

While in her room she heard the front door slam slut. Her mother was home and she wasn't happy. After pouring herself a glass of scotch she came charging up the stairs and burst into Lisa's room without knocking. Lisa was startled, but her teenage anger did the talking.

"What the hell mom, don't you knock anymore?"

"This is my house," her mother said in an irritated tone. "I don't have to knock if I don't want to."

"This isn't your house – this is Russell's house. We just moved in when you decided to marry the bastard."

"Bite your fucking tongue, you little bitch. I got a call today from school. You've been ditching again and you're lack of attendance is going to make you repeat the 11th grade."

"Whatever, I have not missed that much."

Her mother, nearly dropping her drink grabbed Lisa by the hair. Something she had been doing since she was child. In fact she used to grab Lisa by the hair and throw her across the room when Lisa really messed up and her mother was really angry. Every time her mother grabbed her hair it sent Lisa into a panic attack, she started breathing heavy and she tensed up so bad that she couldn't move. Her mother while holding her hair yelled at her and said.

"Look here, I am not going to put up with your shit. If the school is calling me saying that you're missing too much school

then you are. If I'm getting calls from the
school then that's bad."

"I have only skipped a few times, one
with my friends and another couple of
times with Jeremy."

"Are you still seeing that loser?  I
thought I told you not to hang around him
anymore. He's not good enough for you."

"He's not a loser."

"He comes from a poor family and
they live in the bad part of town. He's not
good enough."

"You're one to talk, we've been poor
before. We've lived in the bad part of town."

"That's when you're father left us and
we haven't been that way since then."

Lisa pushed her mother away. Her
mother nearly fell over and had to catch her
balance by grabbing onto the nightstand
and knocking everything over on it. Her
mother gave her a surprised look because
Lisa had never done that before. She had
never stood up for herself before. Her
mother's look turned to anger and then she
walked over and slapped Lisa across the
face.

"You little ungrateful bitch, how dare
you. I'm your mother."

"Then act like it," Lisa replied. "You
don't have to treat me this way. I haven't
done anything."

"You never do what I tell you, you never listen and you don't show me respect."

"You're never sober enough and respect has to be earned. That's what you always told me. How can I respect you?"

Her mother didn't know what to say, she couldn't answer the question truthfully. By that time Lisa's brother had gotten home and ran upstairs to see what was going on. He looked at his mother and Lisa then asked what happened. It was the first time he had ever really cared about what was going on. Most of the time when things got bad he would just turn away from everyone go into his room and listen to music. His mother told him to get out of here. He went in to his room as usual and ignored the rest of the world. She turned to Lisa and said.

"If you don't think I deserve respect then you can get the hell out of here. Get out of my house."

"I'm sixteen years old, where the hell am I supposed to go?"

"I don't care... you get out of my house."

Lisa just stood there in disbelief. They had fought before, but never like this. Lisa just paused hoping her mother would come to her senses or just walk out calling her names while she went to get herself another drink. Her mother didn't do that – she started to scream at Lisa, screaming to get out. So Lisa did, she grabbed some things and left. After a couple of days of staying at a friend's house Lisa came back home only to find that her stuff had been moved out. Her stuff had been given away and her cloths thrown out in garbage bags. She was still able to save those, but everything else was gone.

Lisa just thought that her mother would calm down after a few days and that would be it. It wasn't though. Her mother really had thrown her out for good. The truth is her mother didn't know anything about her daughter except when she was in trouble. The other times she was just in the way or her mother was too drunk to notice her. After 16 years Lisa had just become an inconvenience to her. The loving mother she had once been disappeared.  Her mother lived a shameful life – where there had once been happiness, in place of it was regret and the love that she once had became strength to pour another drink.

Her mother came home to find Lisa going through the garbage bags of cloths. Lisa looked at her and asked what was going on. All her mother could say was that Lisa was not the daughter she had raised and the person she became wasn't wanted there anymore. Lisa sat on the ground sobbing and yelling at her asking why. Her mother simply told her to get out of here before she made a scene in front of the neighbors.

If truth be told Lisa was not even that bad of a kid. She was a little wild, but she did typical teenage things. They were things that wouldn't scar anyone permanently. Lisa's only problem was that she came from an unfortunate family, she was the product of a broken home and there was nothing she could do about it.

Lisa woke from the nightmare she had been having to find the doctor sitting across the bedroom. Dr. Bennett had been there for about 10 minutes listening to Lisa talk in her sleep. Lisa was surprised to see the doctor there in her room, but she has also figured out in the course of being there for a day that there was nothing ordinary in a mental hospital. She looked over at the doctor and asked her.

"What are you doing here?"

"Listening to you talk in your sleep."

"I don't talk in my sleep."

"How would you know if that's true if you're asleep?"

Lisa thought for a moment and gave a dirty look to the doctor. Then she replied. "You have a fair point.

The doctor smiled and replied back. "Don't worry we're not trying to make you crazy, we prefer that you weren't so we don't get the repeat business."

"So why are you really in my room?"

"I sometimes watch the sleeping habits of the patients. To see if they do things like talk in their sleep because it's the best time for the subconscious to release things that a patient would not necessarily tell us if they were awake."

"So did I tell you any truth while I was a sleep?"

"Looks that way! Tell me about your mother."

"What about my mother?"

"You were having a dream about her and from the sound of it; it was a pretty bad dream. Do you have a good relationship with your mother?"

Lisa sat back against the wall and thought for a moment how to answer the question. She didn't want to tell the truth to the doctor. She decided that there was only so much she was actually going to say and she wanted to tell her just enough information to get the session over with.

Lisa replied. "I had an okay relationship with my mother. My mother's dead."

Dr, Bennett asked her "I'm sorry to hear that. Do you think your mother was a good mother?"

Lisa was taken back and a little offended by the question. She paused for a moment. Then she asked the doctor. "What the hell kind of question is that?"

"It's a simple question and when we're finally adults we tend to know the answer to that question. You should already know by now whether you mother was a good mother."

Lisa let out a sarcastic laugh and then she replied. "My mother was married four times, three of them were losers, she was an alcoholic, she never liked anything I did, but she always loved me, and she was always there for me. So yeah my mother was okay. I never had it as bad as some girls that I knew while growing up."

The doctor was taken back a bit by the answer because it was an unusual answer to that question. The answer was filled with such disdain that if it was actually the truth it would be a surprise. She didn't say anything for a moment and just sat there looking at Lisa. Lisa was starting to feel a little uncomfortable by the doctor staring at her, but that was the point - to make her feel more vulnerable so she would answer her questions more truthfully.

The doctor asked Lisa. "Are you really convinced that your mother was a good mother or are you trying to tell me what I

want to hear so you can get out of here
faster? To me it sounds like your mother
was a real bitch."

"Hey, that's my mother you're talking
about."

"If you don't think my assessment is
correct then convince me otherwise"

"What do you want me to say about
my mother- that it was a fairly tale life, a
*leave it to beaver* kind of life? Yes we had
our bad times and my mother could be a
real bitch sometimes like when she was
drinking, but like I said she was always
there for me."

"Does that include when she was
drinking?"

"She was always there for me."

The doctor frowned at the answer.
The she said. "You can put on whatever act
you want – you can hide whatever you want
from me, but the only way you're getting
out here is to start telling me the truth."

Lisa said to the doctor "I have good
memories and bad memories of my mother.
She was wonderful when she was sober and
she was fucking brutal when she was
drunk. When I was teenager she was drunk
most of the time, but when I was a kid I
have nothing but good memories of her."

"That's the most truthful answer
you've given so far."

So that's how it started for them – the truthful sessions between the doctor and Lisa. They started talking about Lisa's mother, about what she was like when Lisa was a child. Lisa even laughed when telling the doctor stories of her and for the first time she didn't feel uncomfortable being there.

The thing about Lisa's mother was she was the nurturing type before she was beaten down by hopeless marriages and alcohol. She was always there for Lisa and never missed a day of picking her up from school. She never missed an opportunity to make her life special. Her mother made every Christmas and every birthday great. Lisa never had one bad memory of her mother until the age of eleven. Even when her real dad left when she was eight years old life with mom was great – she and her brother and sister still had that fairy tale life where every day was wonderful.

When Lisa was eleven years old her mother remarried and that's when things changed. Her mother had finally had enough of being alone and struggling to try and raise three kids on her own so she found a husband, but never bothered to get to really know him. His name was Jack and he seemed decent enough at first, hell it wasn't hard to like him when he bought you things, but that changed. Turned out he was an abusive drunk with the libido of an eighteen year old. Not too long after they were married and everybody was living together the illusion faded away. Lisa's mother would have bruises suddenly appear out of nowhere and after a few black eyes it wasn't hard to figure out what was going on. Of course her mother said it didn't mean anything because accidents happen sometimes. She would make up any excuse so she could get Lisa to stop asking questions and hopefully quell the anger her daughter had for the new husband.

The worst part was the sex; he was loud and abusive with that too. The walls were paper thin in the house so everybody could hear what was going on. Lisa's brother would put his walkman on and drift to sleep to the loud rock music playing inside, ignoring everything that was going on, but not Lisa. She heard it all. Jack wanted sex every night and especially when he had been drinking which was just about every night. He didn't care how he got it either. The only thing he was concerned with was his wife's duties to her husband. Jack didn't see it as rape when he was married to the woman.

After enough times of that routine Lisa's mother discovered that the only way to get through it was to get drunk herself.

At first it was just a few glasses of wine in the evening, but then it turned to the hard stuff. A little bit of whisky made Lisa's mother forget all the endless nights with the abusive drunk she had married. And that's how it started for Lisa's mother. The fairytale did end and Alice came up from out of the rabbit's hole to the miserable life that she had always lived. She eventually did forget to pick Lisa up from school and it happened more than once. Birthdays and Christmas were never the same anymore. Her mother was drunk and passed out most of the time leaving Lisa and her siblings to fend for themselves. And the once comfortable feeling Lisa had at one time for her stepfather changed into disgust and contempt, so much so that she never talked to him unless it was absolutely necessary. To Lisa it was his fault and he was the villain of the sad horror show her life had become.

Her life became a wreck and she did whatever she could do to forget about it. She would experience things most teenagers only heard about – teenage sex, petty crime, and of course drugs. Lisa was a fucking "After School Special" and there wasn't a happy ending waiting at the end of the hour. So after a few years of being married to Jack her mother finally sobered up one day, just long enough to figure out

she needed to make a change and that's
when she packed the car up with a few
belonging and the kids. They left and never
saw Jack again. They moved far away
where their sad sordid life couldn't find
them, but you can't hide the ugly side of
things forever.

It would eventually catch up to them
in a new town, a new house, a new school,
and in a new life. This time it was a man
named Russell- the kind of man that
seemed nice at first and the perfect answer
to a needy family, but they all seem that
way in the beginning. Of course Lisa's
mother would make the same mistake a
third time and after a few months of
knowing Russell she had a third husband.
She met him in bar after falling off the
wagon – how's that for karmic irony. The
third husband moved them into his house
and the same nightmare started again. He
was the truck driver so while he was gone
most of the time the nightmare didn't show
up for a while, but eventually it reared its
ugly head.

Lisa got through telling her story
about her mother up to that point in her
life. Then she stopped and looked away
with tears in her eyes. Lisa blocked
everything out trying to forget the worst
nightmare that she had ever had in her life.
Dr. Bennett didn't want to press the issue

so she ended the session with Lisa. She knew there was something that Lisa was not ready to tell her. It was an important detail about her life that would be a big piece of the puzzle in explaining how she had ended up here. The doctor just looked at her and said.

"We can talk about it next time, you've said enough to me today."

Lisa didn't acknowledge her, but she did glance over at the journal left on her bed that was left by the doctor. Dr. Bennett replied to her as she was leaving the room. "I know you can't say it right now, but try writing it down. It's a good start for you."

# Day 2

Emily arrived at the hospital earlier than usual. She was meeting her boss for breakfast to discuss her latest cases. She never enjoyed these meetings because he always made her feel that she wasn't good at her job because he questioned everything she did. He was like some disgruntled parental figure where nothing was ever good enough, that's the way it seemed. But the one good thing about meeting with him was it made her get better because she would do anything for him not to be too critical. As much of a bastard as he could be he was good at making the doctors underneath him better at their job. He could see things in them that they may not have seen in themselves yet. He was also a friend and always the one person you called when you needed to be rescued. Emily knew that from experience.

Emily waited in her Dr. Carlson's office for a few minutes before her boss finally arrived.  He showed up after awhile with breakfast in hand, muffins, Danishes, and fruit with coffee from Starbucks. He nodded hello as he brushed past her to take a seat behind his desk. He was not one for small talk so he started the meeting. He asked Emily as he handed her a coffee and a muffin.

"So how is the latest patient doing?"

She looked at him with a surprised look because he always wanted to know about her oldest patients first, not the new ones.  She replied back.

"It's going okay so far. Don't you want to know about my older patients first?"

"No need, I've read the reports. You're treatment is good and there is significant progress with all of them."

Again she was surprised; he never gave her that kind of compliment. At this point she was waiting for the other shoe to drop. She didn't want to believe this was happening. She replied back.

"Then what is this meeting really all about if everything with my oldest patients is okay?"

"I wanted to talk to you about you newest patient. Is there anything particular that strikes you about her?"

"I have only met with her twice and we haven't talked all that much."

"But you do have an opinion about her don't you?"

"Of course I do. She is a lonely girl with problems and she was looking for a way to kill herself instead of actually doing it herself."

"And, what else?"

"She's very disturbed with apparent mother issues, which tells me that she came from a dysfunctional family. Her mother was an alcoholic, married a few losers, moved around a lot, and it caused a lot of issues with her. That's all."

Dr. Carlson pulled out a file and passed it to Emily. It was a background check on Lisa. It contained her criminal record, school record, all the places that she had lived over the last 10 years and of course her hospital records including the two times she had been treated for apparent suicide attempts. Lisa hadn't spent that much time in a metal hospital – just a few days so she could be observed, but on a couple of occasions she had seen a psychologist for a while. She saw them until her mandatory time was over and a doctor deemed her well enough to stop her sessions. Dr. Bennett had the look of shock because according to that file Lisa was not well at all and for ten years she had been crying out for help, but no one was really paying attention. In fact she had fooled plenty of people including doctors that thought she was okay.

Emily looked at Dr. Carlson and said. "I can't believe it."

"Now do you understand why she's important?"

"Everybody in this hospital is important, she's not special or anything."

"Maybe not, but she's been sick for a long time and plenty of so-called professionals have missed the signs. It's our job to finally help her."

Emily paused for a moment knowing that her boss was right. Then she asked him the important question. "Why do you want me as her doctor?"

"Look on the next page."

Emily did and that's when she saw it. It hit her like a thunderbolt – the main piece of the puzzle that would begin to answer everything about Lisa. Her mother had committed suicide. Emily looked at Dr. Carlson and said.

"That's why you want me to help her. You think this is the key to her issues."

"I don't know that for sure. You're the one who will have to find out, but I do think that you're the one that can help her more than anyone else."

"Because of my history?"

"There's no one more qualified than you."

"What If I can't help her?"

"You and I both know that the only one that can help her is herself, but someone from similar circumstances going along with her on the journey is never a bad thing."

Emily sighed for a moment then she said. "I don't think it should be me, I don't think I can help her as much as someone like you."

"Well, you're wrong and whether you realize it or not you're already helping her. I hear that she already started writing in her journal."

Emily finished her coffee and muffin and looked over the rest of the file. She knew more of Lisa's history, but that didn't matter, she still had to hear it from Lisa - to get her side of the story. It was the only way Lisa was going to help herself and the only way that Emily could help her. Now it doesn't make much sense to the rest of us, but the only way a person can help themselves is to say their problems out loud, to make them known instead of some figment of their imagination while keeping them hidden inside. Dr. Bennett knew this

to be true more than anyone, not because
she was a psychologist, but because she
had been down that same dark road that
Lisa was going down. And her task would
be to make Lisa talk.

∞ ∞ ∞ ∞ ∞

Emily Bennett watched as her
husband packed his things. She still
couldn't believe it. He was leaving and their
marriage was over. She had never seen it
coming; no matter how good she was at
seeing the truth about other people she
never saw the lies about her husband. He
had been cheating on her for over a year
and it was with his secretary – it was a
fucking cliché and it was worse for her
because she was the poor naïve wife who
didn't know that it was happening to her.
Her husband packed his things in a hurry
trying to get out there before he really had
to explain himself. As far as he was
concerned the divorce papers should have
been evident enough, but he knew how
Emily liked to analyze everything.
Sometimes it was so much so that she
would agonize over the most mundane
detail.

She looked at her husband and asked him. "Why...why do you want our marriage to end? Haven't I been a good wife to you?"

"Yes you have, but it's over and it is time to move on. I'm sorry you had to find out this way."

"You sack of shit, do you know how humiliating it is to get served with divorce papers at work and then find out what everybody else seemed to know about your husband... that he was fucking his secretary and you didn't know it."

"It's bad and believe me I didn't want you to find out this way. I wanted to tell you myself last week, but you were working."

"Don't put this on me. You could have told me plenty of times even if it was three in the morning. Something like this is important enough to talk about in the middle of the night."

"I'm not going to argue with you, I fucked up, but I am still leaving."

"You chicken shit, you never could stand a fight. And how much of cliché can you be. Your secretary, she's not even that pretty and her breasts aren't even real."

Brian, her husband stopped for a moment and gave her an angry look, maybe not, but they're nicer than yours."

Emily shot him a dirty look and then looked down at her breasts, feeling a little ashamed. They weren't bad, but she was not 25 years old either. She wanted to be real, not having her beauty tarnished with something fake.

Emily asked her husband. "How long has it been going on?"

"About a year," he answered. "We started after the office Christmas party."

"Is this some fling, something you need to get out of your system or do you really love her?"

"I don't know, but I have to find out. I know that I don't love you anymore. I could lie to you and tell you some story, but I know how you hate that. I want to show you a little respect."

"You cheated on me and you're divorcing me. I don't think you know the meaning of the word respect."

"You can be mad all you want, but people fall out of love all the time. We had something great once, but I don't feel the same way about you anymore. You shouldn't even fight for this anyway, can you really feel the same way about me anymore."

He was right and she knew it. It wasn't worth fighting for anymore, he wasn't worth fighting for, but she would do it anyway. It wasn't out of loyalty or love - she just didn't want to be alone just like her father. Her mother had walked out on him when she was 11 years old and she saw firsthand the miserable person he had become. Her father had become a broken down bitter drunk - nothing resembling a father and she never became the daddy's girl she should have been.

"I don't understand why you can't give us a chance. We can work things out. I have never been anything but good to you. I never turned down sex. You never had to do the dishes and I never got mad when you wanted to be out with your friends."

Brian looked at her as she was pleading with him. He ignored all of it. All he did before walking out the door was give her a heartless look and then he said.

"I may run from any kind of fight, I may ignore all that is worth fighting for, but I'm not you. I'm not the one who can never let go." And with that said, he walked out of her life for good.

As he was leaving, knowing that he wouldn't hear it anyway, she said to him.

"You can't even be decent enough to say that you're sorry."

That night was the beginning of the end for her. She saw her life as a failure. It didn't matter how good she was at her job or how many people she could help, if she couldn't make her own life happy then what was point to it all. She started to drink. She was never a hard drinker, but she could take it and scotch would do the trick. Emily got drunk and by the end of the evening more than half of the bottle was gone.

She was sitting in Brian's chair in the living room left to her own thoughts, a dangerous thing for a drunk, but that's when the depression kicks in and we do the things that we never thought we would do. Emily was drunk and she was feeling sorry for herself. Her only thought was that life didn't matter and as smart as she was, as good of a doctor that she might be, she couldn't save herself. It's hard to say whether it was the booze doing the thinking or the bad memories that had haunted her for over twenty years. Suddenly it came to her, only one thought, she didn't want to feel this way anymore. She didn't want to feel like a failure and be her father.

Emily got up from her chair and walked into the kitchen. She grabbed the first knife she could find. It was the long one in the sink and it wasn't even clean. Emily took the knife and slit her wrists. The right one first and then the left and for the longest time she just stood there and stared as the blood gushing out onto the floor. She stood there for a good three minutes just staring at the blood until she finally passed out. Emily tried to kill herself and that's what started her on a very dark path into the land of misery. She was just like some of her patients now.

∞ ∞ ∞ ∞ ∞

It was the afternoon already and Dr. Bennett had another session with Lisa. It was the third session since Lisa had arrived at the hospital and Dr. Bennett was already feeling hopeful because Lisa was starting to write in her journal. It was usually the fifth day before any patient did that – most patients had to spend a few days being angry and lashing out at the doctors before they decided to try therapy. In the first few days of being there patients were still trying to figure out why they were in the hospital to begin with. But Dr. Bennett was hopeful about Lisa, maybe a little too hopeful.

Lisa was escorted to Dr. Bennett's office by Randy, one of the orderly's. He was a tall black man that looked scary, but really had a sensitive side and a caring soul. That's why he chose to work at the hospital because he figured he could help people and do God's work as he called it.

"Hello Lisa," Dr. Bennett said to her. "How are you feeling today?"

"The drugs are finally kicking in so that's good."

Dr. Bennett laughed. She then replied back. "They do take some time to kick in and when they do they feel very weird."

"You know this by experience?"

"I wish I could tell you that before you become a doctor, you get to try all the drugs to know what they feel like, but we're not that lucky. When I tell you that I've been where you are, I'm not just saying that. I have actually been there, been given the same kind of drugs as well."

"A doctor with a dark side…nice."

"It's your lucky day. So how is the journaling going?"

Lisa was quiet all of sudden and she paused for a moment, giving Dr. Bennett an angry look. She was hoping for small talk before they got serious, but it wasn't going to happen. She also didn't know how to answer the question. She decided the truth would be good enough.

"Look doctor, let's get something straight. I know why everybody thinks I should be in here, but I don't need to be. I had a bad day a couple days of ago. A glass of wine and good night's sleep would have made it okay."

Dr. Bennett interrupted her before she could say anything else. "A bad day is what you have at work. You tried to kill yourself, that's a little more than a bad day.

It means you're hurting and that you have a bad life."

Lisa shot Dr. Bennett an angry look again. She said. "Call it whatever you want, but I'm going to do just enough to get out of here in ten days. I'll write in your stupid journal, I'll tell you a few details about my life, and I might even cry. We all have a bad life, but unlike most people in this place, I can still function and will go on functioning in ten days."

"You're going to have to be honest with me to get out of here and you're going to have to talk about things you may not want to. If you don't want to play ball then you'll be here a lot longer than ten days. So yes, let's get something straight, Lisa, I'm the only one that can determine if you're really getting out of here in ten days."

Lisa finally sat down and it was a good five minutes before she said anything. Dr. Bennett just sat there with her notepad and pen waiting. She picked a spot on the couch and poured a glass of water from the pitcher on the coffee table. She drank her water and waited  trying to make the doctor feel impatient and say something. She also wanted to let the doctor know that she was in control. Finally Lisa spoke up.

"What do you want to know?"

"Do you have any major family issues that have bothered you over the years?"

"No, not really. Everything is peachy with my family."

"So your mother committing suicide didn't bother you at all?"

Lisa paused again, surprised that Dr. Bennett even knew about that. She asked. "How did you know?"

"We have your file with a background check. You're listed as the person who identified her so your name is on record."

"Okay my mother committed suicide, so what."

"So how about you answer the question, did it bother you?"

Lisa said in an angry tone. "Of course it bothered me, it was my mother, she was dead and she did it to herself. That doesn't mean my life is in shambles because it."

"That's the third time since we've met that you've said that your life is not bad, who are you trying to convince me or you?"

Lisa didn't speak for a few minutes again. Dr Bennett finally spoke and said. "I told you - you will have to be honest to get out here. If you want to be silent that's fine. You can stay here as long as you want until you're ready to be honest."

Lisa replied. "Fuck you Dr. Bennett."

"Well that's a piece of honesty. Tell me about your family. Do you have any brothers and sisters?"

"I have a one brother and one sister."

"Are you close to them?"

"Not really. I have not spoken to my brother in four years and my little sister, well; I talk to her about every couple of months. She stays on the road a lot."

"What does she do?"

"I don't know, she tells me that she's in a band and on the road with them. Although I think she's just a groupie looking for free ride."

Dr. Bennett got up to pour herself a cup of coffee. She asked Lisa while putting cream and sugar in it. "Why haven't you spoken to your brother in four years?"

Lisa sighed, a little angry at the question because she didn't want to answer it. Finally she did. "He's a selfish asshole that doesn't care about anybody but himself. He makes good money, has a live in Chinese girlfriend with two kids, and would rather have lots of money, lots of nice things to keep him entertained so doesn't have to deal with family. That about sums him up."

"Do you try and stay in contact with him?"

"No, there's no point, he doesn't want to talk to me and I'm not going to keep trying with him. He has my phone number. He can call if he wants."

"How do you feel about that?"

"Here we go, the question about how I feel."

"It's a relevant question, how do you feel about it. Are you okay with it, are you angry…are you glad that he doesn't talk to you."

"How do you think I feel, he's my brother and it's a fucked up situation when the only family you have doesn't want to talk to you."

"Yeah it is and whether you realize it or not it affects who you are and what you do."

"How do you know that? You could be wrong. Why can't it be that I am just pissed off about it and that it doesn't affect my life in any way?"

"True…it can happen, but do you really think that's true for you?"

Lisa went back to not saying anything again. Dr. Bennett sat there waiting with her pen and her notepad. All Lisa could do in her anger was to sit and stare at the clock, waiting for the session to be over. She silently tapped the arm of the chair to the exact beat of the seconds on the clock as they passed slowly away into the maddening silence that filled the room.

Finally Dr. Bennett broke the silence and said. "I obviously hit a nerve. Don't you think it's time to quit wasting our time together and tell me the truth!"

# DAY 3

Lisa was having breakfast alone as usually when Rose walked over and she sat down. Lisa said hello, but Rose ignored her while having a conversation with herself. Rose was rocking back and forth whiling counting with her fingers as she talked.  It was hard to make out what she was saying, she just kept saying over and over, "1 is infinite possibilities, I'll try, but I won't succeed. It's over now. 1 is infinite possibilities, I'll try, but I won't succeed. It's over now."

Lisa asked Rose. "Are you really crazy, I know it's an unusual question for a place like this, but I thought I would ask?"

"Crazy is a relative thing."

"Let me ask you this, are you what they consider crazy, or are you just misunderstood?"

"Misunderstandings... aren't we all in this place? They don't know what they're talking about. You do though."

"What?"

"You know what to say when they ask."

"Okay I think you're just talking gibberish now."

"Maybe, maybe not – how would you know if you're crazy?"

Rose smiled at Lisa with this conniving smile that had the look of something being planned. Lisa just gave her a dumbfounded look, but didn't know what to say. Rose broke the silence.

"Crazy is a relative thing ...truth is beauty, beauty is truth. There's your answer."

Rose was just spewing out intangible words that on the surface appeared to make no sense at all.  At least this is what Lisa was thinking, but she was paying attention and Rose let her know it.

"Rose looked as if she was possessed and about to let her in on some great mystery. She looked at Lisa eye to eye and gave her great monologue.

"You search for answers, but look in the wrong place. You want to know what to say to set yourself free, but you look in the wrong place. Courage, you may have only when you can look past, present, and future. Your conundrum… can only be considered crazy? Just when you think you know that's when you don't know anything." Rose tapped her index finger on Lisa's forehead as she finished her last line. Then she smiled at Lisa and turned away.

She turned away repeating the same line over and over, "1 is infinite possibilities, I'll try, but I won't succeed. It's over now." Lisa had an eerie feeling come over her. She didn't know what to say so she sat there eating her breakfast slowly while watching Rose looking away and repeating the same words over and over.

∞ ∞ ∞ ∞ ∞

Lisa was escorted to her fourth session with Dr. Bennett.  It was her third day in the hospital and by all accounts the longest three days of her life. That was the way she felt because she had never talked this much about her family before especially with a stranger. There was no mistake about it, Dr. Bennett was a stranger; no matter how much she tried to be a friend to Lisa she would still be a stranger. The doctor was running a little bit late so Lisa was made to wait for her in the doctor's office and she felt uncomfortable. Lisa still had not warmed up to the idea of speaking with the doctor about personal issues. She was scared even though she tried to hide it and just because they had a repore with one another didn't mean that Lisa could tell all of her darkest secrets to the doctor.

Dr. Bennett arrived a few minutes after Lisa was escorted to her office. She said hello and they both exchanged pleasantries before they got started. Lisa sighed for moment, took a deep breath, and asked the doctor.

"So I guess you want to hear more about my relationship with my brother and sister and the lack there of?"

"No not today," Dr. Bennett said. "Unless you want to tell me more than you did yesterday.

"No, not really."

"I thought today that we would talk about something else."

"Such as?"

"I want to talk about your previous suicide attempts."

Lisa gave her an angry look and then she said. "I've already told you that I have never tried to commit suicide."

"That's not what your hospital records say – you tried about ten years when you were in college and you were hospitalized for it. You were under suicide watch."

"Yes I was hospitalized, but they were the ones that said I tried to commit suicide and had me under watch for it. What happened to me was an accident."

"Believing the lie is never going to help you."

"It's not a lie, don't you think I'm smart enough not to fail at a suicide attempt."

"A lot of smart people who try to commit suicide fail at it and sometimes they do it for good reason. They do it because they're trying to get attention, because it's a cry for help."

"That's those people. I'm not one of them. I don't care what your file says."

Dr. Bennett looked at Lisa and started shaking her head at the same time in disbelief. She couldn't believe that after ten years Lisa was still in denial, but the only conclusion she really had was that Lisa had utterly convinced herself that it never happened. Dr. Bennett picked up her medical file and read what the doctor's report said about the suicide attempt.

Lisa was twenty years old when it happened. She was in her second year of college struggling to pass all of her classes since she had missed a lot of school due to being laid up after a car accident. The car accident that had happened two months before caused her to be in a brace for broken foot for a month. She couldn't drive and she couldn't really get around on her own so she had spent a month with her mother, so she could help while being laid up. Finally she got to go back to her life at school even though she was still in a brace and had to walk with a cane. One of the things that she got from the hospital were pain killers, vicodin to be exact, with instructions on how many she could take on any given day for the pain. After two months she was already on a refill and had about ten left.

She was sitting home alone, stressed out, trying to figure out what she was going to do about school. She was failing and didn't know how to catch up enough to pass her courses that semester. But there was something else bothering her from the stay at her mother's house. It was something that she couldn't forget no matter how much she tried. So there she was, alone in her apartment, crying and wondering what to do. She tried to find a solution to it all. She tried not to feel ashamed and dirty over what had happened at home. No matter how much she thought about it, there were no solutions and no way out. That's what Lisa thought.

Lisa scratched off the label on the bottle of her pills and then grabbed a handful out of the bottle, not really counting and then she swallowed two or three at a time until the pills in her hand disappeared. She passed out, barely alive when her roommate found her. The paramedics were called and Lisa was rushed to the hospital. When they found her all the pills from the bottle were gone. The hospital resuscitated her, pumped her stomach to clean out her system, and saved her from certain death. Lisa woke up a couple days later and it was a few day after that before she was allowed to leave.

Lisa had to see a doctor like Dr. Bennett. They needed to make sure she wasn't completely crazy before letting her go and to find out why she tried to kill herself. Lisa kept telling them over and over that she wasn't trying to commit suicide, she just didn't realize how many pills she took and the bottle didn't have a label to tell her. That was her excuse; it was clever to have deniability or to just convince herself that she wasn't trying to commit suicide. The doctor in the hospital didn't believe it and the condition for her release was that she had to do weekly counseling at the hospital – she had to get routine checkups to make sure she wasn't going to do it again. The checkups only lasted for one visit and after that she disappeared not even having contact with her mother for six months. The last part wasn't in the file, but that's what happened no matter what Lisa tried to convince herself of.

After Dr. Bennett was through reading the report in the file she looked over at Lisa who was trying to ignore her. Lisa didn't want to hear what was in the file, the lie that she had created was still easier to cling to. Dr. Bennett finally asked her.

"Now do you believe what happened?"

"Anybody can write lies on a piece of paper in a file, but you weren't there, you don't know the truth."

"Do you?"

"What kind of question of that?"

"It's a valid one because what I see in this file is a cry for help and you've had it for too many years."

"Is that your expert opinion?"

"It doesn't have to be an expert opinion from a doctor to be the right opinion. Now why don't you tell me what happened then."

Lisa went back to her silent treatment, staring off into some corner of the office, ignoring the doctor after she asked a tough question. Dr. Bennett tried to tell her that it was childish to keep doing that, but Lisa did it anyway. As far as she was concerned they were going to do these sessions on her terms and she would only answer the questions she wanted to answer, not the doctor's. After a few minutes of silence Dr. Bennett asked another question completely unrelated to what they had been talking about.

"So if I call your brother and tell him what happened to you would you like that?"

"Fuck you doc."

"Good you weren't just ignoring me."

"I don't see what happened to me back then as being relevant. It happened, I got better and I went on with my life."

"Do you feel that your life really got better after that?"

Lisa gave Dr. Bennett a dirty look and then fell silent again, but this time she didn't wait a few minutes to answer. Lisa replied to the doctor. "Look I graduated, I started a career, I've been successful at what I do, and I have a happy life. What more do you want?"

"Tell me about the personal relationships you've had since then except your brother and sister."

"What do you mean?"

"Tell me about your friends, your boyfriends, were you ever engaged, are you or have you ever been in love? I want you to tell me about the personal relationships you've had since then and tell me how they affected you life."

"Fine. All my friends from college live in other states and I don't ever see them – a Christmas card is about all we do. I was engaged once, I cheated on him by accident and he wouldn't work it out with me so we broke it off. I've had one other boyfriend since then who wanted me to be something I wasn't and we broke up, but we try to be friends."

After a long pause from Lisa, Dr. Bennett asked her. "Do you have any friends that you hang out with?"

"Just coworkers; sometimes we go out for drinks and do dinner parties, but that's it."

"Are any of these people somebody you would consider as a best friend?"

"Not really, but they are fun to hang out with sometimes."

"Do you have any pets?"

"I have a small dog. She's cute and loveable, but a cute ugly. She only likes me because I put food in her bowl."

Dr. Bennett sighed because she was looking for a better answer, but she got the truth and it wasn't that good. She looked at Lisa with a sad look and said. "You're the perfect lonely girl."

Lisa was floored by this, completely surprised by the comment. She replied back. "You don't know what you're talking about. I have a life...I have great life."

"Do you, because it sounds like to me you have nothing in your life that you truly care about. You could take or leave it and when you have nothing in your life worth fighting for then you're a lonely person."

"That's just your perception doctor."

"True, but it's my perception that will allow you to leave in ten days."

"I thought you said that it's up to me to get myself out of here in ten day."

"It is, but you still have to convince me that you're ready to leave."

Lisa didn't say anything for a moment. She picked up the glass of water on the table in front of her and took a few sips. It was the first time she had ever taken a drink of water during the session. Dr. Bennett thought it was kind of interesting that she would chose this particular time to finally take a drink – was she really thirsty or was she finally letting her defenses down so she could do the therapy for real without fighting it.

Lisa continued to stay silent, but this time the doctor didn't press her to say anything more. It was almost time for the session to be over and Dr. Bennett marveled at the fact that Lisa did need something even if it was something simple like a glass of water. The doctor ended the session five minutes early and then prepared her notes for what she wanted to talk about the next day.

On the way back to her room Lisa drifted into memory losing all sense of her surroundings and time. She didn't even know where she ended up in her memory. All of it was like a constant stream of nothingness and the only image she saw was herself swimming along a blank canvas struggling to keep from drowning in the blank images along the way.

∞ ∞ ∞ ∞ ∞

"Mom, you're not listening to me." Lisa shouted through the phone. "You weren't there; you don't know what he did so how do you know if I'm lying or not?"

"Lisa, it doesn't sound like him; I can't believe he would do such a thing."

"Mom it's always hard to believe until it happens, but you need to know what kind of a person he really is."

"You're upset with me so you're making up things about him just to get back at me and I won't stand for it."

"Jesus fucking Christ mom, you never listen to me. If Sara told you this, you would listen and do something about it."

Her mom started crying and then screamed at her daughter through the phone. "You're a selfish little bitch and you never appreciate anything I do for you. I would never allow any man in my life to hurt you."

"How can you stop it if you're never around or you're too drunk or high to even know what's going on?"

"You're sick and you need help. Tell me where to send a check and I'll get you the help you need."

"Mom you're the one who needs a wake-up call, he's not good for you and you need to get rid of him before he hurts you."

Lisa's mother didn't say anything else; she just slammed the phone down and hung up on her daughter. All Lisa could do was lash out in a fit of rage and then it turned into crying and then silence. She couldn't believe her mother would take his side and flat out, call her a liar and that's when she finally realized that her mother didn't care about her at all.

At that moment when everything seemed clearer than ever although everything was far from it Lisa sat and started to think about her life being over. She poured herself a glass of vodka and

then poured the bottle of painkillers out
onto the coffee table. One by one she
swallowed a pill with vodka, not even
realizing how much she was taking. All she
wanted was the pain to stop. It was the
wrong kind of pain for the pills, but she
didn't care. The truth of it was she wanted
everything to be gone and upon realizing
that notion that's when she knew what she
was doing. Lisa eventually passed out and
the next time she woke up was in the
hospital with her stomach pumped and a
doctor asking questions.

# DAY 4

**T**here was screaming coming from the living room as the young girl woke from a deep sleep. It was her parents fighting and it was getting physical again. Most of the time it was just shouting matches between her parents, but every once in awhile, when her father was really drunk he would hit her mother and she defending herself would hit back causing a bigger fight. It was one of those nights and the young girl knew it from the unstifled sounds coming from the other side of the bedroom door. The girl got out of bed and went into her closet shutting the door until she couldn't hear the sounds anymore. She would go in there to get away sometimes falling asleep until the sounds of silence were all that was left. About thirty minutes later it was over and the last sound that muffled through the doors was the front door of the house slamming shut. Her father had left in anger and for a moment all the young girl could think about was that her drunk of a father had left for good.

The young girl got out of the closet and walked out of the bedroom to find her mother crying in the kitchen while at the same trying to clean the blood off her face. She smiled at her daughter when she saw her emerge from around the corner into the kitchen trying to act like that everything was okay. Her mother had a knack for shielding the scary moments that occurred when she fought with her husband. She never wanted her daughter to see the horrors of the home front, but the young girl knew the truth. She was about to be eleven years old and she knew what drugs and alcohol could do to a person – she even knew about sex and all the dark things that came with it. However her mother still saw her as a little girl; still innocent and naïve.

The young girl asked her mother. "Is everything alright mom?"

"Everything's fine dear."

"Your bleeding again, did he hurt you bad?"

"Oh this is not from your father. I know you probably heard us fighting, but your father would never do something like this to me."

"Why do you lie for him?"

"You don't know what you're talking about?"

The young girl looked at her mother in anger and with a few tears in her eyes. She said. "Screw you mom, you shouldn't have to lie for him. He's a bad person and he shouldn't be here."

"How dare you? Don't you talk about your father that way. He's still a good man."

The young girl was crying now. She replied back. "Don't defend him, you don't deserve this."

Her mother got up out of the chair she had been sitting in and walked over to her daughter. She kissed her on the forehead and said. "Don't cry my dear. Everything will be all right in the morning." The young girl tried to smile, she wanted to believe her mother, but she had seen too many bruises and broken dishes to believe that everything was going to be okay.

Her mother smiled again and told her. "Tomorrow when everything is fine again we'll go shopping and have a girls day out. It will be you and me, just the two of us and you'll forget that any of this ever happened." The young girl went back to bed trying really hard to believe her.

So morning finally came and she walked out of her room to find her father asleep on the couch and her mother gone. She waited for an hour in the hopes that her mother had gone to get breakfast or to bring her some kind of surprise since it was her birthday. Through all the commotion of the night before the young girl had forgotten that her birthday was today and through some small hope she wanted to believe that her mother was taking her shopping.

It didn't happen that way, her mother never came back. The young girl was left with a drunken father who never had a kind word to say about his wife ever again. He also didn't know how to raise a daughter, all he knew was how to drink and hate anybody that had ever wronged him, which cast a shadow over any of kind of a home life for the young girl. To this day the young girl, now a grown woman, is still waiting for her mother to come home and spend the day with her. She is still waiting for the next day when everything really will be okay. It is that painful memory that makes Emily wake in the middle of the night with a fear that she has never been able to make go away.

∞ ∞ ∞ ∞ ∞

Lisa woke up to her roommate staring at her while sitting on the edge of her bed.

It was early; the sun wasn't even shining yet. Lisa asked her roommate, Lisa of Earth, what she was doing.

Lisa of Earth said. "I am supposed to give you a message from the visitors."

"You mean the visitors from the planet you're from?" Lisa replied.

"Yes, they want me to tell you that they are coming for you, but you can make them stop with the code."

"What code?"

"It's a certain piece of information."

"What information?"

"You have it and they need it."

"What if I don't know the code?"

"You must know it if you want to survive?"

Lisa stared at her roommate in shock because she didn't know if she was threatening her or trying to warn her. It could go either way, after all she was crazy, but the aliens could be a metaphor for something else. One never knows in a place like that. Lisa asked her roommate.

"Are they going to kill me if I don't know the code?"

"Kill is such a dirty word, but it would be better for you to know the code."

"Can you protect me?"

"I can only stall the inevitable."

Lisa of Earth went back to her own bed after saying that. There was nothing more to say because she was simply a messenger as she constantly pointed out. Lisa didn't know what to make of what she had been told. She was afraid, but at the same time laughed it off, or tried to. She thought to herself, it couldn't possibly be true. Then she turned away to go back to bed with her thoughts racing and focusing on the fear that was building inside of her waiting to erupt.

∞ ∞ ∞ ∞ ∞

Dr. Bennett got to work early and was told that her boss was looking for her. She went by his office first. He was having breakfast as usual and looking through case files, making his notes and signing patients release forms. He asked her.

"So how's it going with your patient?"

"Which one?" Emily asked her boss.

"The one that thinks that she's not trying to commit suicide."

"Everything's fine."

"Really?"

"Yes, I am making some progress."

"Where are you in your sessions – what are you talking about?"

"I have found out some family history and yesterday we started talking about her first suicide attempt in college."

"Good. Did you find out the real reason she tried to do it."

"No, not exactly. We ran out of time yesterday, but I did figure out that whatever happened had something to do with her mother."

"That's good, but you need to get details, find out exactly what happened."

Emily gave her boss a funny look. He had never asked these many questions before about a particular patient and there shouldn't be any more trust issues with her since completing her probationary period after her trouble with alcohol and drugs. This patient was different somehow and she couldn't understand why he was so interested. She asked him. "Why are you so interested in this patient, you've never taken this much interest before in one patient."

"It's going to be a tough case and I want to make sure you're on top of it."

"We've seen cases like this before; we have more than one patient like her."

"I'm not worried about you're clinical skills, but I am worried about your personal attachment to a case like this."

"It's just another case."

"That's good that you see it that way. What can I say - I'm still worried about you. You've done a lot to keep yourself together over these last few years, but it always takes one case to make us lose our objectivity and become emotionally involved."

Emily smiled and thanked him, but she also told him that there was nothing to worry about she could handle this patient no matter how difficult it might be. Her boss smiled at her. Then he said.

"I did find out some other information about her that will be useful."

"What did you find out?"

"Apparently she was married about seven years ago. It only lasted a year before they got a divorce. Looks like he won most of their stuff in the settlement."

"Do you know the reason for the divorce?"

"He claimed she was having an affair and that the child she was carrying wasn't his."

"Was it ever proven?"

"No, she had an abortion before they could find out. There's something else though, she was committed to a hospital for a month and was under suicide watch. Apparently she had some sort of breakdown at work, but we can't find out any details of what happened."

Emily had a look of horror on her face. It was one more piece to the puzzle with this patient and the doctor was beginning to see how tragic Lisa really was.

"I guess we'll have something else to talk about today. Emily said to her boss.

"I would say so. Please try to get the truth out of her today about her suicide attempts. Her ten days are almost up and if she ends up staying here it could be for a long time. She needs to really work with us so we know how to get her better. I don't want just another patient resorting to drugs so they ignore what's really wrong."

Emily agreed with her boss. It was a hard case and time was not their friend. Lisa could easily be a drugged up lifeless patient in their hospital who would never leave. She had that potential unless they got her to really start dealing with her problems. Dr. Bennett went to her office to make some notes before her next session with Lisa.

∞ ∞ ∞ ∞ ∞

The day was going by quickly and the afternoon had finally arrived – it was time for another session with Lisa. Dr. Bennett in addition to her notes that she made about her in the morning also made a decision, she would try something different to see if she could get Lisa talking. It may not be nice, it may not even be ethical, but the last few days had been most a waste of time for both of them so Dr. Bennett decided to try something drastic. Lisa arrived and took her usual seat on the couch; it was the same place that she had been sitting for the last few days. It was familiar and that's why she sat there – she needed something familiar because whether she would admit it, she was scared of being in a place like the hospital.

Lisa sat down and immediately said to Dr. Bennett. "I'm still not going to tell you what you want to know."

"That's up to you, but you know how this is going to work. If today was your tenth day you wouldn't be leaving the hospital. You're not ready to leave because you haven't made the effort to work with us."

"I'm not sick and no matter what you tell yourself, I don't need to be here."

"If that's what you want to believe but as your doctor, I kind of have the final word on that. Today we are going to do something a little different."

"What's that Doc?"

"I'm not going to ask you the same questions, because you won't tell me if you don't want to. What you're going to do is this. I am going to say certain words and you have to respond without thinking about it. Just say the first word that comes to mind.”

“That's all you want me to do?”

“Yes, but there's more. Any response you give me that I feel like is disturbing we talk about and you have to answer my questions – honestly.”

“What if I don't want to play?”

Then the session is over and we start medicating you and eventually we'll do electric shock treatments to help get you regulated. By the time we're done with those kinds of treatments, a month will have gone by and you'll be so wasted that you won't feel a thing or know what day it is.”

“You can't that.”

“Sure I can – if I deem it necessary for the proper treatment of whatever mental disorder you might have then I will.”

“And if I just sit here saying nothing.
“

Dr. Bennett looked towards the door and shouted. “Orderly.”

The Orderly walked in and asked what the doctor needed. She told them the patient's session was over and to take her back to her room and put her in restraints. Lisa gave Dr. Bennett a horrified look. She couldn't believe it, the doctor wasn't bluffing.

Lisa replied. "Fine we'll play your stupid game."

Dr. Bennett started with her list of words. At first they would be simple words, just random things that we never think about, but are still important. She looked at Lisa and said that she was ready to start.

"Okay here we go," Dr. Bennett said. "Food."

"Necessary."

"Movies."

"Entertaining."

"Beer."

"Good."

"Car."

"Expensive."

"TV."

"Nice."

"Love."

"Overrated."

Dr. Bennett looked up and gave Lisa a sarcastic smile. There was a pause in the wordplay game so Dr. Bennett could see if Lisa was going to say anything else about love. She didn't, Lisa just gave the doctor a dirty look. So they started again."

"House."

"Residence."

"Family."

"Good for some people."

"Brother."

"Bastard."

"Apple Pie."

"Grandmother."

"Mother."

"Bitch."

"Husband."

"Waste of time."

"Marriage."

"An even bigger waste of time."

Dr. Bennett stopped and looked at Lisa with very serious look. Then she asked. "Do you really think that about marriage?"

"Is that what you really want to know about me?"

"It is for now. I think it's interesting that three most important things that I mentioned were the things that you think are overrated and a waste of time. So yeah I want to know why."

Lisa paused for a moment and then responded. "I don't know anything about love or marriage, but it seems to be overrated and a waste of time if all it can cause is pain in someone's life."

"Have you never been in love before?"

"No."

"Even when you were married?"

Lisa looked surprised, but tried to hide it as she replied. "I've never been married."

"Are you sure you want that to be your answer because lying isn't going to help you at all."

"I'm not lying."

"We already know that you were married once for about a year. We found out in your background check. Marriage records are public records."

Lisa gave Dr. Bennett another dirty look – it was getting a little old trying to hide her past with Dr. Bennett already knowing certain things about her. She replied to the doctor.

"Why do I need to answer these questions if you already know the answers?"

"Because I want you to tell me everything and be honest."

"I just don't see the point in talking about stuff when you can find it out for yourself then make your evaluation from that"

"What you tell me is more important – your version of your life is always better than what I can read in a file. That's why it's important to talk, but it only works if you tell the truth."

"So you keep saying."

"I shouldn't have to keep telling you that. All we seem to do is waste more time."

Lisa poured herself a glass of water and took a sip while pausing again. She wanted to waste more time and she wanted the doctor to know that she was in control of the time spent with her. So they waited as nobody said anything and Lisa just sat on the couch drinking her water. Dr. Bennett sat in her chair tapping her pen on the notepad in her lap. It was a constant routine and battle for control. It was hard to say in this little exercise who really won – was it Dr. Bennett for not seeming desperate in trying to get Lisa to talk so she could save her in ten days or was Lisa showing the doctor that she didn't have to talk about her life if she didn't want to. Finally Lisa spoke up. She asked the doctor.

"What do you want to know about my marriage?"

"Why did it end," Dr. Bennett asked her.

"He cheated on me."

"You know that for sure?"

"What's that supposed to mean?"

"How do you know that he really cheated on you? I want to know the story behind it and if you actually got proof. Tell me the details

"Fine I will go back to the beginning."

Lisa just sat back and started to tell the story of her marriage. She married young and she married the first guy that seemed to truly care about her. They were both twenty three, just out of college and ready to find success in the world. They were both convinced of the idea that being married would somehow add to their success. He wanted to settle down or at least he thought he did and she was looking for an escape, but for Lisa it was a delusion that she convinced herself of so she didn't have to face the truth. All she wanted was the appearance of someone caring about her and someone that she didn't have to care about at all. It was her escape from a family that had lost all sense of emotional sincerity and just walked around under the delusion of happiness. With Lisa and her family there were a lot of delusions like happiness and love.

Her husband was a software designer trying to invent the next big thing in the computer industry that would make him rich and famous. He adored Lisa, but he had never been in a relationship before her so he had nothing to compare it to. Lisa was basically the first girl that really seemed interested in him. They dated for the last few months of their senior year in college and then one day after graduation he surprised her with a ring. She didn't know what to say at first, but after a pause she said yes. He was a nice guy, good looking, sincere, and wasn't that bad in bed. She certainly had been with worse.

The important thing was she was getting away from her family by using the excuse of marriage. She even took it a step further by moving to Chicago for his career. So they moved and the fairy tale like romance ended two months later. He worked long hours and she was bored. Of course she had her career, but it was something to occupy her time from 9 to 5. Even when she was with her husband she was still bored and couldn't figure out what would make her happy.

Lisa became moody and she wasn't easy to be around so her husband worked even more hours as so he didn't have to go home to his wife. It's important to know that he was a good man and although his name isn't important how he treated Lisa is. He treated her well despite the fact that he was annoyed with her. He never did anything to hurt her, he was always there for her, and he took care of her, which is more than one can say about most men in that situation. It was never good enough. Lisa would have an affair with a complete stranger six months into their marriage. She met him at the local coffee shop she frequented every morning on her way to work and she never bothered with his name. They flirted with each other and they causally fondled each other in public when they saw each other every morning. It started out innocent, but things like that rarely ever end that way. Finally one day he convinced her to go home with him and skip work. She gave in and did just that. So for a few weeks they met each other on their lunch breaks and fucked liked crazy in his apartment. Lisa would end it a few weeks later and never saw him again.

To this day Lisa could never figure out why she did it. Maybe she just wanted to have someone else love her even if it was in some trampy way. Maybe it was an escape from the same old routine that she had always known. Then again maybe it was a tragedy that she needed because she just couldn't live with any kind of happiness – it made her numb and uncomfortable. A few months later she was at an office party with her husband. Lisa didn't know anybody that well because she was never interested in getting to know anybody from his work. During the party she noticed a beautiful young woman that her husband seemed to be good friends with. But instead of seeing a good friend in the co-worker, Lisa a saw something else out of jealousy. Lisa saw the woman as her husband's mistress and the reason he wanted to work late – it was far from the truth. Truth wasn't something she was used to because she couldn't see in herself. It was easier to blame someone else instead of face the hard reality about the person she really was and it's a theme in her life that has never left.

After the party was done Lisa picked a fight with her husband and accused him of cheating on her even though she didn't have any proof. Of course that was something that she didn't admit to the doctor. Her husband moved out that night and every bad thing that could be said to hurt one another was said that night. He called her a conniving bitch and she called him a liar. But who really was the liar in that relationship? That's what Dr. Bennett was beginning to wonder. Six months later she was divorced from her husband and moved back to her hometown never speaking to him again. So there it was the sad ballad of Lisa's failed marriage and it seemed to have happened a lifetime ago.

After Lisa was done telling her story Dr. Bennett looked at her and asked.

"Did you ever get proof of his affair?"

"No, but I know my ex-husband and I know what he did."

"Did he ever know about your affair?"

"If he did he never said anything about it, he never used it to get back at me and he said every hurtful thing you can think of to make me feel bad."

"Do you ever miss him?"

"Why would I he's my ex-husband."

"You can still love your ex-husband. You can still remember the good times you've might have had."

Lisa gave the doctor a curious look. She didn't know about the doctor, just a few details, but the doctor was willing to give up something of her own personal experience to empathize. Lisa took advantage of that because she wanted to know if the doctor was full of shit or truly genuine. She asked Dr. Bennett.

"Do you have some kind of experience with this?"

"You mean do I still care about my ex-husband?"

"Something like that."

"I do...I always will in some way because he was my first love. No matter how much he broke my heart or treated me bad a part of me will always love him."

"Do you remember any good times with him?"

"I have to in order to see him as a good person. If I can't see that in him then I'll hate him forever and that makes me a hateful person. We had some good times, I can't lie about that."

Lisa just sat back on the couch keeping silent again as she drank her water. Instead of waiting for her to say something and start the session again Dr.

Bennett decided to ask her some more questions. She asked Lisa.

"Have you ever had any successful relationships?"

"I never got married again?"

"You don't have to be married to have a successful relationship."

"Isn't that the end result though?"

"I would think being able to love someone completely without understanding and then to give yourself unto a person without any guilt or fear would be the end result. I think just being able to be with somebody like that is success?"

"That's a long description."

"Perhaps, but the real question is, am I wrong?"

"I guess not – it sounds good to me."

"Have you ever had something like that?'

"No."

"Not Ever?"

"I've never had something like that before."

Dr. Bennett put her notepad and pen down then got up to pour herself a cup of coffee. She wanted to make Lisa feel like that it was no big deal to answer these questions by acting like that questions were routine because she knew that the questions were about to get more serious, even hurtful. The doctor was trying to avoid a negative reaction to the questions she was about to ask, but there was no telling what could happen with Lisa. The doctor needed to understand where Lisa was coming from – what her true motives were. Obviously it had nothing to with love and that was part of her problem.

Dr. Bennett looked at Lisa with disappointment and said. "I don't buy any of this B.S. with you. You play the part of the victim, but perhaps it's really you that causes others around you to be the victim."

"Why would you say that?"

"It's true isn't it?"

"Fuck you; you don't have a clue of what you're talking about."

"If I'm wrong then prove me wrong."

"What can I say that would make you believe me? You seem to have your mind already made up."

"Look at from my point of view," Dr. Bennett replied as she leaned forward in her chair. "You tell me that you've never been in love, yet you got married."

"Lots of people get married without being on love," Lisa interrupted.

"Maybe, but while you seem to have never loved him, he did everything in the world for you and you didn't care. He did everything to make you happy and it wasn't good enough. You cheated on him and then accused him of the same thing as if you had any right to do so. But you didn't have any proof – you let you're assumptions cloud your judgment. And in the end he left without you ever trying to fight for it."

Lisa looked at the doctor with an angry look and replied. "I don't see what your point is."

"You wanted to be the victim. You only married him because you didn't want to be alone and you wanted to get away from the family that doesn't seem to love you. But no matter what you wanted you caused him to be the victim. And he was the victim of your cruel selfish desires."

"He was the one who took advantage of my love for him." Lisa said as she started to shed a few tears

"Stop it. You can put the act on all you want, but it's not the truth is it?"

"I did everything for him and he cheated on me."

"You cheated on him, how are you any better than him?"

By this time Lisa was already standing up and pacing the room. She was angry – she was confused. She had convinced herself of so many things that it was hard to see what the truth really was. Maybe there wasn't any truth at all, just a nightmare that she had been sleeping through and had never woken from. Lisa replied to the doctor.

"You're the one being cruel Dr. Bennett."

"For telling you the truth, that's not cruel. It's an act of kindness if anything else; lying to someone is cruel. It's never the right thing to do. I'd ask you if your mother ever taught you that, but it's not hard to figure out the answer."

"My mother has nothing to do with this."

"She obviously does. Everything about you is because of her."

"That could be said of any child."

"Maybe, but its more true in your case. She never loved you did she?"

"She was my mother, of course she loved me."

"But you don't really think that. She was supposed to love you because she's your mother and that's what mothers do. Although you can't say for sure whether your mother ever really loved you, there's no evidence of that, no clear cut answer, and that's what your great fear is."

"My great fear, what the hell are you talking about? I don't have any fear about my mother."

Dr. Bennett leaned back in her chair and cracked a smile. She wasn't laughing at Lisa, but she was amused at the fact that Lisa couldn't see the obvious. But we're all victims of our own delusions and their usually the ones that we create in order to tell ourselves that everything will be okay – that we can be happy." Dr. Bennett replied to Lisa.

"No, you don't have any fear about your mother. You're afraid that no one can love you and if anybody does then you convince yourself that it's all a lie. Those that love you must be trying to hurt you."

"You're wrong," Lisa said. "You're not even close to being right."

"Lisa you keep saying that, but you have yet to prove me wrong."

Lisa got angry and knocked some of the stuff off Dr. Bennett's desk. She stared at the doctor, but Dr. Bennett also wasn't surprised at Lisa's anger. The doctor let her cool down for a couple of minutes. Lisa turned around and looked at the doctor in an apologetic tone then asked her.

"Why are you pushing me like this?"

"Because I want to find out the truth and I need to know if you actually know what that is."

"But would you believe me if I told you?"

"Why don't you try me?"

"How can you believe someone who's the victim, but causes others to hurt?"

"Are you asking me a question or giving me a statement?"

Lisa sighed and paused for a moment. She wanted what she was about to say to be perfect, to make sense so the doctor could understand. Lisa didn't want any confusion because she was trying to make a point. The point was, Lisa knew more than what she was letting on about; she was in control more than what she wanted the hospital to know. But she was still hurting and the hurt was beginning to boil over. She said to the doctor.

"If you're a victim then you don't have any control over what you do, right?"

"That's true to a certain degree, but we always have a choice."

"But you do agree that there's a certain amount of control that we lose when we're a victim of our circumstances."

"Yes, I do."

"Then it would be fair to say that if I do this," Lisa took the sharp end of a pair of scissors and slit her left wrist. "I don't have control over what I'm doing because I'm a victim." Lisa then took the scissors and slit her other wrist while blood dripped from the other wound onto the tiled floor leaving a small puddle of blood. Dr. Bennett was horrified at what just happened and the expression on her face confirmed it. And Lisa, she just stood there giving a dirty look to the doctor as if to say, *fuck you I can do what I want.* Within moments Lisa fainted

and fell to the floor into her own pool of
blood. Dr. Bennett was frozen in shock, she
couldn't even yell for help because she was
so horrified at what Lisa just did.
Fortunately the orderly outside heard the
commotion and came inside the office to see
if everything was okay. Lisa was taken to
the infirmary and Dr. Bennett was helped
to her chair, but she wouldn't say anything
for about an hour. She was too afraid to say
anything. Nothing like that had ever
happened with a patient under her care
before.

# DAY 5

**E**mily slept in her cloths on her own couch. She couldn't find away to get past what had happened. Never had she been faced with something like that, not even in her darkest moments as an alcoholic and drug addict. All she did was go home and fall asleep thinking about the events that had happened during the day. But when she awoke the next day somehow, someway she put herself together and went to work. It was a new day and that's what she told herself.

She got to work early and the first place she went before going to office was the infirmary. Emily had to check on Lisa; to make sure that she was okay and to see if her treatment would have a setback. She waited in the infirmary for over an hour to see if Lisa would wake up, but she had been sedated as an extra precaution beside the restraints. While she was waiting her boss came by. He was looking for Emily and figured that she would be there checking on Lisa. He said hi to her and then asked her.

"So did you actually get any sleep last night?"

"A little, I slept on the couch if that tells you anything."

"I've had a few nights like that in this job."

"Look if you want to take me off her case, I understand, but this could've happened to anybody."

"That's true, but I'm not here to punish you. It's a set back...that's true, but you're also getting close."

Emily looked at Dr. Carlson who was sitting next to her in the waiting area of the infirmary. She gave him a surprised look – it was hard to believe she was getting close to anything except to destroy the last fragments of sanity Lisa might have. She asked him.

"What I am getting close to. The patient tried to kill herself and I pushed her over the edge. That doesn't make me a very good doctor."

"On the contrary, you hit a nerve and it must be pretty close to the truth. Now that you've hit that nerve you can work with her on the healing that she will have to go through. She's living with some serious pain and you can start to help her to get through that now."

"I don't know how good I can really be. I don't know where to even begin at this point."

"You do what you always do – the mind is a puzzle and you work with the clues or the pieces you get to put the big picture together."

"I know that she feels like nobody can ever love her and I think that there was somebody else besides her ex-husband that got through to her, but it ended badly and made her even worse."

"You may be right and here are a few other clues. The nurses found some Polaroid pictures in her purse and on the back of one them it says from Jake with a date from a few years ago."

Emily looked at the Polaroid pictures. One of them was a picture of a long road covered by trees and alongside the road was a stone wall with a house in the distance. Emily could only assume that the picture was of Lisa's home. Maybe it was her childhood home or the place that she lived now, but it looked like a home for Lisa. The other picture was of Lisa cast in a shadow within the perfect light. She had a half smile and was bathed in innocence. It looked like that whoever shot the picture caught her at the right moment. It was beautiful picture, but it was a sad picture. And what made it sad was the inscription on it – *to my beautiful lonely girl I will always love you.* On the back was the inscription from Jake with the year the photo was taken. Emily and Dr. Carlson both concluded that Jake must have been very important in her life. However it was the photos which were the most important items because they were a clue into Lisa's soul, her pain, and her tragic life. And if a picture is worth a thousand words then these pictures were must have been a book. Emily looked over at Dr. Carlson and asked him.

"So what do you think these pictures mean?"

"I don't know, there sad pictures so I assume there is some tragic incident behind them."

"Lonely is the word that sticks out in my mind more than anything else."

"It's a powerful word. Hell we're all lonely in our own way, but I think the meaning behind it can best be answered by Jake, whoever he is."

"He may not want to be found and if he is then he may not be any help because it is her."

"True, but you can't ignore the possibility that he's the key."

"The key to her salvation?"

"No, not like that, but the key to what really happened to her. It's been my experience that troubled and lonely people always find someone to confide in even it's a stranger."

"Let's just hope he didn't cause her to be a victim."

"Something tells me that it won't be that easy. There's a more complicated story behind the photos and what he was in her life."

∞ ∞ ∞ ∞ ∞

Lisa finally woke up, the drugs were wearing off and the pain hit her hard like a falling brick. As she reached up to rub her head because of the pain she realized that she was restrained. It was the moment that she finally realized the gravity of the situation and that she had let the darkness come inside one again. Dr. Bennett walked over to check on her and said hi. Lisa couldn't say anything. She was terrified and she was angry – there were no words to say, but her silence said everything.

Dr. Bennett let her know that she was going to be okay and that the stitches in her wrist could be taken out in a couple of weeks, but there would probably be a scar on both wrists. Lisa nodded to acknowledge the doctor, but she still wouldn't say anything. She didn't want counseling and this would be a good time for a session since it was a setback – that's what she assumed the doctor was thinking. Sometimes we just want to be alone after something bad has happened and this was one of those times for Lisa. Although this time there wasn't going to be any counseling, in fact it was time for the cold hard truth.  And it was for both Lisa and Dr. Bennett. Dr. Bennett looked at her with a serious look and said.

"I think it's time you and I had a serious chat. I'm not going to counsel you and this isn't a normal session. However I need you to listen up, which means I really need you to listen to me"

"Do I have to talk?"

"No, I get to do the talking this time."

"Good."

"I'm sorry if I pushed you – that was my intention. I needed to find a breaking point. Sometimes in my job we have to do that. This is a setback for you and you're not going to be leaving in 5 days. You're not ready and this stunt of yours proves it."

"All because of you – you shouldn't badger emotionally unstable people. You never know what they're going to do."

Dr. Bennett smiled. It was the first time Lisa admitted that she was unstable in some way. She replied to Lisa. "I'm glad to hear you admit that you might have problem."

"I never said that. Believe what you want to believe."

"Whatever. The truth is doctors sometimes forget that we can cause problems for our patients too. That happens when we push too hard. I don't regret what I did, but I'm sorry for the result. You know it occurred to me last night that I didn't act any different than most people in your life."

"What do you mean," Lisa asked with a look of curiosity on her face.

"You don't feel like anybody ever loved you or for that matter respects you. You think people look down on you or never take you seriously and when people get to know you they never see the real you. When that happens people treat you wrong and take you for granite."

"You could be right."

"I know that I am." Dr. Bennett said to Lisa with a sincere look on her face. I know that now, but there's something else that you may not realize."

Lisa who had been looking away while Dr. Bennett had been talking turned her head to face the doctor. She was curious now about what the doctor had to say as if it was some great insight that no one had ever told her. It wasn't – it was the truth and that was something no one had ever bothered to tell her either. You only get told the truth by someone who cares; for those that don't, they don't tell you the truth because it's not important to them. Dr. Bennett was trying to cross the divide, to finally be someone that cared enough to tell Lisa the truth, but not as a doctor, as a friend. Lisa looked at the doctor laying in her hospital bed, her hands in restraints and said.

"So what don't I realize?"

"You're not much better than those in your life who never cared to tell you the truth. The only difference is they know why they don't, but you can't figure why you can't tell the truth about anything when it's staring you right in the face. You're just as much of a liar as everybody else, but you don't know why. I bet you have this debate inside your head whether it's out of revenge or self pity."

Lisa had a horrified look on her face, surprised at what she was hearing. Dr. Bennett had kind of an angry tone, but really the doctor was just being direct. Lisa responded out of anger.

"What the hell is you're problem. Are you out to kill me? You can just push me over the edge and eventually I'll kill myself. What kind of plan is that Doc?"

"Hey I got to take advantage of the fact that you're in restraints, but you need to hear this." Dr, Bennett paused for a moment while Lisa turned her head away out of anger. Lisa couldn't get up and walk away like she wanted to. Dr. Bennett began speak again.

"You can look away all you want, but it doesn't make a difference. I am still going to tell you what you need to hear. Our job as doctors is to help our patients get better by confronting their fears...by confronting their problems and learning how to deal with them so they can function again. But the only way to do that is to get at the truth. I can ask you all sorts of questions such as what do you really know about true love. All you seem to want to do is dodge the question or tell me some basic story that I would get from watching a movie on the Lifetime channel. But do you really know what it means to love someone completely without judgment only to have them break your heart so bad that all you think about is escaping from everything you know... finding that suicide is a better answer than to go on living. I can ask you about your mother, but all you will tell me is that she never understood you and that makes her an unloving mother. Well I got news for you all daughters feel that way about their mothers at some point. But do you know what it really means to have your mother show you that she didn't love you. How about when your mother walks out on you the day of your birthday and a drunken father has to raise you, but doesn't know how. Then you find out years later that your mother created another family and raised her children in that family, but you were never good enough to be a part of it. And to add icing to the cake you never found out why because eventually your mother would kill herself before you could reconnect with her. Lisa that's real pain and you may have it, but how do I know that when you won't tell me. The thing is I can't help you unless you tell me the truth. That's the part you have is this performance. It's the compromise you have to make in order to get out of here."

Dr. Bennett pulled out the black and white Polaroid photos and showed them to Lisa. She turned around to see what the doctor had for her after Dr. Bennett asked to her to look at what they had found among her belongings. Lisa had a look of shock when she saw the photos. Dr. Bennett said to her.

"These are some interesting photos – both beautiful and sad. If I ask you about them I wonder what kind of story I would get. I wonder why you're referred to as the lonely girl in one of them."

Lisa said. "You had no right to take those photos from my things. They have nothing to do with any this."

"Then why do you care so much about me seeing the photos."

"They're none of your business."

"I think they're important and they have relevance to this situation. The thing is Lisa I can find out things about you from other people such as Jake." Lisa's face had a look of terror now at the mention of his name. "But I'm only going to get their versions of what happened to you," Dr. Bennett replied. "I can't know what happened in your life just like the story behind these photos unless you tell me the real story and your version."

"What if I don't?"

"There won't be any more sessions until you do and at the end of ten days they'll keep you here for a very long time. It's up to you. I'll see you tomorrow." Dr. Bennett patted Lisa on the hand and gave her a smile trying to tell her that it would be okay if she wanted it to be. Then she turned around and walked out of the infirmary.

∞ ∞ ∞ ∞ ∞

Dr. Bennett stared at the black and white Polaroid photos lying on her desk for about half an hour. She was trying to piece the puzzle together. The photos were important and Lisa's look of shock when she saw that the doctor had found them confirmed that importance. Since she didn't have a session with Lisa that day she decided to do some detective work – she need to find out who Jake was and what he meant to Lisa. The best place to check was the contact list in Lisa's cell phone. It was among her things when she was brought into the hospital. Sure enough she found an entry for someone named Jake.

She called the number and a guy answered. It was Jake and after a few minute of talking she found out that he was an ex-boyfriend of Lisa's. Jake was surprised to get a call from the doctor, but he wasn't surprised that Lisa ended up in a mental hospital. He explained to Dr. Bennett that he always believed that one day she would end up in one. It was an odd comment, but also full of disdain. Dr. Bennett concluded that their separation must have been done through a lot of anger. It was probably a very bad breakup and he wasn't completely over it yet. She needed to know more about Lisa and wanted his version so they agreed to meet for coffee.

Dr. Bennett met Jake at a coffee shop about a block away from his web and graphics studio in the downtown part of the city. She introduced herself and he was gentleman, buying her a cup of coffee while trying to make an awkward situation a little easier. After she ordered her coffee he looked at her with a serious look and asked.

"So you're the Psychiatrist treating Lisa – is she going to be okay?"

"I don't know yet. She's only been at the hospital for a few days."

"What happened, how did she end up there?"

"She was arrested after trying to get a Middle Eastern store clerk to shoot her because she was threatening him. A judge ordered her to be treated for ten days to see if she needs to be in a mental hospital, but that's all I could tell you."

"It figures that she would be forced to go in there. She can't just get help on her own."

"Why do you say that?"

"She'll never admit that she has a problem. In her mind she's perfectly okay and is not living with any pain. It's also not the first time she's put herself in a situation where she could be killed."

Dr. Bennett looked at Jake with a surprised look and asked him. "Are you saying that she wants to die and instead of doing it herself she tries to get other people kill her instead."

"Yeah something like that," Jake said. "She's catholic so suicide is a mortal sin, but it's okay if someone kills her. I felt for a long time while we were together that she didn't want to live. It's always been too painful."

Dr. Bennett took a notepad out of her purse – she made a note about what he said. The she asked him how they met and how they were together. So Jake told her the sad sordid history between him and Lisa. They had met four years ago by accident. She had just moved back and he was just starting his new career. When he started his company she was the one agent who helped him find a building for his new studio. Lisa moonlighted as a commercial rental agent for extra money – she would find people great commercial property for a finder's fee in her friend's rental agency.  It took a few weeks to find the right place. In her spare time a lot of their days were spent

together looking at buildings and so a lot of
dinners happened between them. It was as
if they were already dating because during
those few weeks they got to know each
other really well. It also didn't hurt that
when she needed to move all of a sudden to
a new apartment he was there to help her
when no one else could. It just so happened
that they became really good friends and
started dating for real.

Jake explained that right from the
start he knew that there was something
tragic about her, but she was fun and she
made him laugh. That was all he needed so
he stayed with her. And it was good for a
few months until her tragic life hit them
both square in the face. Jake and Lisa were
out to dinner and they ran into one of her
friend's husband. He was a nice guy, but
when she saw him a terrible memory that
she had repressed came back to the
surface.  In a public place she told him and
his wife to fuck off and when he asked what
was wrong she screamed out loud for all to
hear –"you raped me, that's what's wrong."
It was shocking to hear and no one knew
what to do in that exact moment. Even
Jake was stunned and froze from any kind
of action. Finally the restaurant manager
broke the mood and asked everybody to
leave.

That night Lisa told Jake what happened. It was a party about six months before that and they were all doing shots of whiskey. Lisa couldn't hold it down very well and passed out drunk. At some point when things were getting a little too erotic for a party – people were swapping partners; her friend's husband took advantage of Lisa. She woke up to find him taking off her pants and underwear. Lisa didn't have the strength to fight him off – all she could do was let out a soft toned "No," but of course he didn't listen. He would have his way with her, he raped her more than once and all she could do was force herself to pass out again hoping to forget what happened. Of course she did confront him about it the next day and his excuse was he was drunk. The most embarrassing part was that he had the nerve to ask Lisa not to tell his wife. After that she repressed the memory and acted like it never happened, but she also never saw the bastard again. I guess when she finally did the memory couldn't stay hidden and so she lashed out in her own true fashion.

Lisa told Jake all of this and she also told him she couldn't see him anymore. She didn't want to date or have a relationship – she wasn't in a place within her life where she could do that. It was bullshit and it was just an excuse not to try so she didn't have to be hurt again. It was the story of her life, but the funny thing was she actually went out of her way to try and find that special someone. She was hoping that one day she could find love again and she searched for it constantly – she did things like online dating and letting her friends set her up on blind dates.

Oh she would tell herself that she didn't want to find someone that she didn't need someone in her life, but her actions spoke differently.  Jake knew all of this and he refused to walk out of her life because people had been doing that to her since she was a little girl. He cared a lot about her and felt sorry for her. In fact he loved her; he admitted to Dr. Bennett that he had fallen in love with her after only a few months because she brought out something good in him. She made him believe again in love and brought out hope – something that he had forgotten in the many years since his heart had been broken the first time. He wanted to be that person for her because she needed someone like that.  She didn't want to lose him because Jake had become a great friend. So that's what happened – they remained friends and they became best friends. Not a day would go by that Lisa and Jake wouldn't talk to each other. He opened up his life and family to her; his family accepted her as on their own, a long lost member that had finally been found. Lisa didn't have a family of her own anymore. Her mother was gone by that time.

She had killed herself about a month after Lisa and Jake had met. Jake did meet her once and to tell you the truth he wasn't that impressed. She was a fake; nothing seemed real about her and she was angry about everything in her life. To her everything was a disappointment including her children. The odd thing was Lisa didn't seem that broken up about her mother killing herself. Her brother acted like it never happened – one day she was there and the next day she wasn't. That's all he cared to know about his mother dying. Lisa's little sister Sara just blamed Lisa because their mother had always been disappointed with her. Jake commented that meeting her family was like something out of Joyce novel. And Lisa, well, she didn't really mourn her mother. She just went on with her life except that one important detail. That's when Lisa decided she couldn't be with Jake anymore, at least in a romantic way.

Jake and Lisa both tried dating other people. For Lisa it never lasted but a few dates and there certainly wasn't any sex involved. In fact she had given up on that part of her life – it just didn't interest her.

Jake on the other hand never seriously dated any woman for the next couple of years. He just had his sexual excursions – it was never serious, but it was the physical part of a relationship that he could never live without. So after a couple of years and failed attempts of trying to have a relationship with other people Lisa and Jake  decided to have another go at it – they were going to try and date again. And why not they thought to themselves – their lives were so much a part of each other's anyway; everybody thought they were already married. So it started again – this time with a simple question that Jake and Lisa asked each other, why they weren't dating. But like all things that seem good at the time they usually don't end up that way.

The second time around lasted for about a month before Lisa would put an end to it again. This time her excuse was simple, Jake wasn't the person she was looking for. She told him that he couldn't measure up to what she really wanted even though she wasn't clear on what that was. He wasn't good enough for her and he didn't make enough money to suit her lifestyle. That's what she told him. The only thing is she never knew how much money he really made or what he was worth. Lisa let her assumptions dictate her thinking and like anybody who has intimacy issues she believed her own false notions about what could make her happy. She broke it off and they argued until all they could say were angry words to each other. They tried to talk about it until all they had was contempt for one another. And that was it. Jake called her an uncompassionate bitch and walked out for good. They hadn't spoken to one another for eight months. Of course they had been there before where they got mad at one another and had to cool off for a few days. They wouldn't talk for a few days and then would laugh about it later because they thought they couldn't live without each other. Turns out they were wrong and the last words that had been spoken to each other really were the last words.

Dr. Bennett made her notes and let Jake get it all out. As Jake told the story there was an angry and contemptuous tone in his voice. She could tell that that he was still mad at her and couldn't feel sorry for her. Lisa had hurt him bad and he wasn't over it. Jakes finished his story by saying.

"I don't know what else I can tell you. She's a very lonely person and she carried a lot of pain with her. I am probably not the most objective person when it comes to talking about her."

"It's okay," Dr. Bennett said. "Sometimes it takes us a long time to get over a really deep hurt caused by someone that we love. If you didn't care it wouldn't hurt."

Jake smiled at her and said. "I guess I can't really hide that from somebody like you. I still care about her and hope one day that she can finally be happy, but I also want her to hurt for while. Does that make sense?"

"Yes, it's understandable, but I think you can help her too."

"I think I'm the last person that should try and help. I said some pretty awful things the last time we spoke. One thing in particular that I don't think she'll ever forgive me for."

"What did you tell her?"

"I told her that if I were her mother I wouldn't love her either and that it also doesn't matter who tries to love her because she's too delusional to believe it anyway."

"Wow, that's pretty bad. You don't really believe that do you?"

"I do and I don't. There is a certain truth to it.

"I'm also curious to know she thought you weren't good enough."

Jakes sat back in the booth and sighed for a moment. He had already been too hurtful to Lisa and didn't want to do anymore to her. But he told Dr. Bennett the truth, at least what he saw. He said.

"It came down to money and a lifestyle. She makes really good money through her two jobs and she never thought that I made enough because I didn't make her salary."

"Did she know how much you made or how much your company was worth?"

"No. I never told her because it wasn't any of her business. I knew how much she made. Lisa spent a lot of money on things and wasn't really good at saving money. I on the other hand don't like to spend it and budget everything to the penny. I'm a business owner; we have to be that way to survive."

"Do you think she couldn't understand that about you?"

"Yes and no. Her concept of money was if you have it then you can spend it on nice things, but when she was running out of money she would get in her thrifty mode. Lisa would budget and start saving money. She would ask for advice about money because she put herself in debt and then later accuse me of lecturing her on her finances when it wasn't any of my business. I do believe that there were a lot of concepts that she didn't understand when it came to money, that's just my opinion.  And in the end she felt like I wasn't good enough and I couldn't take care of her because she never really knew my finances. At least that's what I saw."

"Money and sex always change everything in relationship. Are you worth more than she is?"

"Yes I am, but I never told her because we weren't in a serious relationship yet. That's the way I felt and until you get to that point, the money conversation doesn't exist yet. But I never wanted her to like me because of money. Call me crazy, but I always thought money shouldn't matter."

Dr. Bennett laughed and then replied. "It would be nice if it didn't, but that's never the case, at least that's what I've discovered. Did she ever give you a reason why money was that important to her?"

"She told me one time that she never had any money growing up. Her mother always had to marry a man with money so they could survive. Also I think it has something to do with the fact that she didn't have any kind of help with college. How she got to where she is today she did all on her own."

"Lisa's got more money now than she ever did and she doesn't want to be dependent on other people or have them dependent on her especially when it comes to money." Dr. Bennett said as she gave Jake a concerned look.

"Yeah, she also said that before. It's like she wanted me to know it and always remember it. She even told that the worst kind of woman was one that needed to depend on a man or have them depend on a woman."

"Jake, that's not uncommon by someone who's never been their own person and is trying to escape what they've always known. I can tell you that it's not you personally; Lisa would be that way with any man she was with. It's an issue that no man can solve - she's the one that has to fix it."

"It may not be personal, but I'm the one who's lived with it while being friends with her, it doesn't get much personal than that. "

Dr. Bennett smiled at Jake and said. "Perhaps you're right. I need to go, thank you for meeting me and for the information. I still think you should see her – you can help whether you believe it or not."

Jake replied. "How long is she going to be in there?"

"A judge will make a determination based on our recommendation in four days. But in my opinion she won't be going anywhere unless she can find acceptance and understanding in what she's become.

Like I said, you might be able to help her so she doesn't have stay there longer than four days."

Jake smiled and said. "I'll think about it. If I choose to help then I will give you a call."

"Just don't wait too long.  Don't let your anger make your decisions; I'm sure you're better than that. Forgiveness is the best way to find healing." Dr. Bennett walked out of the coffee shop and Jake sat there in the booth pondering what she said. He knew she was right, but he still had to work through the anger in his own way and right now spite was his best friend.

# DAY 6

**D**r. Bennett arrived at work early and before going to her office went to see her boss. He had something for her. It had arrived late and it was Jake who had sent it. There was a note attached to the package and it said,

Dear Dr. Bennett

Here is something from Lisa. She gave it to me as a present. It's a painting that she did in an art class while in college. I figure you can use it more. It might help you with her. For Lisa this is how she has always seen the world. It's a beautiful painting; she always did have a lot of talent, but its proof of how sad she really is. Maybe you can help her find some happiness again. I certainly couldn't do it.

~ Jake

Emily looked at the painting and sighed. It was a painting of a girl looking out through a window with bars on it. It was a symbol of the prison the girl had created for herself. It was a prison that Lisa had created and she was trapped looking for a way out. She just couldn't admit it yet. Emily was looking at the painting and seeing a very big piece of the puzzle. Dr. Carlson just looked at it and said. "I think you know where this is going with her and what you have to do."

Emily replied. "Yes I do. The painting is a cry for help, but you know there's something pretty interesting about the painting."

"What's that?"

"You don't see the girls face in the painting – its means the person in the painting can be anyone of us."

"You're right, Dr. Carlson said. "The biggest enemy we have is the nameless face that carries all of our pain and haunts us forever."

Emily smiled at his profound statement. The painting did have an answer within it, but only somebody outside of Lisa's life could see it. That person right now would be Emily.

∞ ∞ ∞ ∞ ∞

Later that afternoon Dr. Bennett had her session with Lisa. It was her first session since she cut her wrists in the doctor's office. Dr. Bennett had a nervous feeling because she didn't know how it was going to go especially after she had found out so much about Lisa from an old friend. And of course she saw the painting that Lisa had done in college – her view of the world. She knew the session would be awkward, but necessary because time was running out. She was trying to help Lisa and didn't want to see her spend the next few years in a real prison even if it was in the form of a mental hospital. Lisa was better than that, but it would be up to Lisa to stop what might be inevitable.

Lisa walked in the office and took her usual seat on the couch. Dr. Bennett smiled at her and asked. "So how are you feeling today?"

"I'm not as tired. The drugs were making me tired."

"That's what they're supposed to do. They also try and prevent you from killing yourself. You can't kill yourself in your sleep can you?"

"I guess not, but if there's someone that can, that's the person I want to meet."

Dr. Bennett smiled at Lisa's comment. At least she was getting her sense of humor back -the drugs hadn't affected that yet. Then Dr. Bennett officially started the session by saying.

"So I met Jake yesterday."

"How was that," Lisa asked with a surprised look on her face.

"He seems like a very nice guy. Why didn't it work out between you two?"

"He left, he didn't want to be my friend anymore and I can't help that."

"What happened to make him leave?"

"I don't know. One day he wanted to be with me and then the next he didn't so he left."

"And he didn't give you a reason."

Lisa gave the doctor a dirty look and replied. "It doesn't matter what he told me. He was mad and he left."

"Lisa the reason always matters. He must have thought that his reason was good or he wouldn't have left. Now tell me why and don't tell me that you don't know because I think you do."

"Fine he told me that he couldn't love me and that nobody would ever love me."

"Do you think that's true?"

"No, anybody can love somebody if they let themselves do it."

"What about you, have you ever let yourself love someone?

"Yes."

"Was it Jake?"

"I'm not going to tell you who it was. It's not relevant."

Dr. Bennett got up out of her seat and poured herself a cup of coffee. She told Lisa that it didn't matter what she thought was relevant, the doctor would use whatever information that might seem helpful and ultimately in the end would determine what was relevant or not. She also told Lisa that she wanted to hear her side of the story about Jake. He was important to her at one time and was a big part of the story surrounding Lisa's journey to this place in her life. She looked at Lisa with a serious tone and said.

"I need to know the truth about him and what he meant to you. Over three years is a long time to be together and then all of sudden he just walks out. There are important reasons behind that."

"Look he was my best friend, but friends come and go and our time together was over."

"Did you fight for him when he walked out?"

"No."

"Why not, was he not worth it?"

"Sure he was, but sometimes people are meant to be in your life for a while and then they go."

"How do you know that he was one of those kinds of people?"

"He would have stayed and not walked out."

"But you shouldn't have to fight for it, is that what you're saying?"

"What...this is ridiculous, it doesn't make a difference if I fight for it or not. If he was meant to stay then he would have."

D. Bennett smiled a little bit and then said. "But you can't say for sure - maybe you were meant to fight for him and then he wouldn't have left. Then he wouldn't be one of those people in your life that's only there for a short time. But you can't bring yourself to do that can you?"

Lisa shot the doctor angry look. The doctoring was pushing again and those same thoughts of killing herself so she wouldn't have to listen came back, but she didn't anything, not this time. What she did was scream in anger, however, and then she said.

"Quit making his problems about me. They were his problems, not mine and I can't help if somebody hates me and walks away. Why would anybody want to fight for something like that?"

"Lisa people who love each other get mad at one another and we all have those thoughts that maybe it would be better without that person. But then we realize that it's better with them and that's when we fight for it. You give up way too easily – just because something makes you mad for a little while doesn't mean it's bad for you. People can annoy each other, but they get over it."

"I only give up on the things that aren't worth it and he proved that he wasn't worth keeping in my life."

"What makes you say that? I've met the guy and all I see is someone that loved you, for who you were, someone that would've done anything for you. He was someone that was there for you no matter what. Something like that doesn't come along very often Lisa and when it does you hold on to it because it's worth fighting for."

"A guy will do anything for you if they can have sex with you."

"You don't really believe that about Jake do you? Let me ask you this. How many guys in your life did what he did for you? How many would have gone through hell and back to make you happy?"

"I've had a few that were nice and helped me a lot when I needed it."

"That's not a good enough answer. Did you ever have to call him at 3 in the morning to come help you?"

"Yes I did, a few times."

"Did he ever tell you no. I bet he was there every time with no excuses. I bet he put his life on hold to help when you called those times.”

Lisa just looked at her with a sad look. She didn't want to answer the question. She was trying to ignore it, but mostly she was trying to hold back the tears that were welling up in her eyes. Dr. Bennett looked deep into her with a penetrating look searching for the truth and trying to get Lisa say it out loud. She asked Lisa.

“Was he there for you no matter what when you called at 3 in the morning?”

“Yes he was.”

“Then for the love of god why was he not worth fighting for?”

“He made me mad sometimes. He could be irritating?”

“Was he supposed to be perfect?”

“No one is ever perfect?”

“Those annoying qualities about Jake, did they out weight the good things about him?”

“I suppose not.” Lisa said, starting to get choked up. She was nervous and agitated all at the same time because she was being forced to see the truth about Jake.

“Then you really don't know why he wasn't worth it do you. Did you just not want to be with him?”

“I didn't want to date him.”

"Why – did he not have anything you were looking for in boyfriend?"

"Money, he didn't make enough. He didn't make as much as me?"

"Do you even know how much money he made?"

"Not really, but I could tell by the way he lived he didn't make that much."

Dr. Bennett started laughing at Lisa. She smiled at her and shook her head in disbelief. The one constant thing that she always saw in patients was there willingness to believe something under false assumptions. Lisa was no different and she was somebody that had been living a lie for so long that it seemed she had started to believe it. She looked at Lisa who was getting annoyed at the doctor laughing at her and said.

"You know it's easy to believe a lie when we only believe what we tell ourselves."

"What is that supposed to mean."

"It means that we convince ourselves of a lie when we're too afraid to accept what we don't know. You don't know for sure how much money he had and you were too afraid of the unknown so you believed the lie that you convinced yourself of. But what's even sadder is that you convinced yourself that how much money someone made should determine your relationship."

"Money is very important and most guys can't handle a woman making more. It's causes problems besides I'm not going to have anybody be financially dependent on me."

"Yes money is important to a degree. But again, here you are with your poor assumptions – in the three years that you knew Jake did he ever ask you for money, make you buy something for him? Did you ever pay any of his bills?" Dr. Bennett said to Lisa with a stern look.

"No. If we went out he took care of the bill most of the time. The only times he didn't is when I wanted to do it myself. Even when we were friend he always did that? He seemed to be able to take care of himself and never tried to rely on me."

"So money wasn't really an issue. You were just afraid of what you didn't know. Money is always a great excuse and it can cause big problems in a relationship but admit it he wasn't that guy who would have screwed you out of money or ruined your life."

"He didn't appear to be, but I've been wrong before."

"There was something else and that was your reason for not fighting for him."

"You're searching for something that isn't true doctor."

"I don't think so. What was it about Jake, why couldn't you be with him? Why did you let him walk out of your life?"

"I already told you, he didn't want to be friends anymore and I can't stop that."

Dr. Bennett looked at Lisa with a stern look. She was trying to make Lisa uncomfortable or nervous with the hope that she would finally tell the truth. She said to Lisa in forceful tone."

"You're not telling me the truth. You caused him to walk out. Why."

"I didn't do anything."

"There was a reason and you were the reason why, now tell me the goddamn truth." Dr. Bennett said in an angry tone.

"I just didn't want to be with him in that way and he wouldn't let the issue drop. He argued with me trying to get me to say something. He was looking for an answer that wasn't there and I kept trying to tell him that there wasn't any other answer. I just didn't want to be with him."

"So he didn't believe you. The answer you gave was an excuse; it wasn't the real answer, right?'

Lisa started to cry and her words were filled with tears. She didn't know what to say, she was searching for an answer, but that's when she found it. In the midst of her anger and her pain she found the truth – the truth that she had hidden deep inside, the truth that she wanted to forget. She said to the doctor.

"Maybe there is more to it, but I didn't give him a wrong answer. He didn't want to accept what I was saying."

"*A wrong answer*, so there was more than one answer. What was the other one?"

"I didn't mean it that way."

"What was the real answer?"

"There wasn't one."

"Yes there was."

"Doctor you believe what you want to believe."

"Damn it Lisa, if you're not going to be truthful after all this then get the hell out of my office. We're done and you can spend the next few years here."

Lisa was stunned. Dr. Bennett had gotten angry before, but not like this. The doctor was accepting defeat, letting Lisa suffer without offering any more help. It was a strange feeling coming to this kind of breaking point when your doctor finally gives up on you and you know that there's no one else that will help you. Lisa screamed in anger again. Then she asked.

"What the fuck do you want from me... nothing I tell you seems to be good enough?"

"I only want the truth - it's what I've always wanted from you."

With more tears in her eyes Lisa said to Dr. Bennett. "I was scared."

"Scared of what?"

"I was scared that he wouldn't love me just like everybody else in my life."

Dr. Bennett smile at Lisa. She said. "Now that's truthful. Is that why you pushed him away?"

"Yes, he would've eventually left me and it would all be for nothing."

"But you don't know that for sure?"

"Maybe not, but it always happens, why shouldn't he be the same."

Dr. Bennett looked at Lisa with a heartfelt look. She understood now because she had lived that fear too. Dr. Bennett walked the same dark road where fears collide with poor assumptions. She said to Lisa.

"There are no guarantees except what we choose to believe and that goes for lies as well. The only thing we can do is take a chance because without doing that we'll never find happiness. The real question for you is, can you live without him knowing that he might have left because of a lie and that you could have stopped it?"

Lisa gave Dr. Bennett another sad look and said. "I don't know." And that was it the session was over. It was a break through. For the first time progress had been made and Lisa could admit a certain

truth out loud, but there were still some
truths buried deep down waiting to come
out.  But that was for another day.

# DAY 7

**E**mily arrived at work early, she was having breakfast again with her boss and this time she had good news. She had a break through with Lisa and she wanted to tell her boss that things were good. She had not been able to do that in a week. Dr. Carlson walked in his office and prepared something to eat off the food cart in his office. Emily took a seat and before he could ask she just said it.

"We had a break through with Lisa yesterday."

"That's good, what happened."

"I found out the real reason her last relationship ended and why she couldn't be with him."

"This is that Jake fellow, the one that was her best friend and took the photos."

"Yes, and he was right about her. He didn't just tell me a bad story about her out of anger."

"What's your opinion of her or should I ask, do you share his opinion of her?"

"A little bit. She is a lonely girl and she has lived a life based on lies."

"Well that's not uncommon for a depressed person. They usually create a perception that nobody loves them."

"With Lisa though, it's not that simple. There's something more to it. I think there is a very specific...ugly reason that she's created that perception and lived with it all her life."

"Keep plugging away and find out what it is?" Dr. Carlson smiled at Emily while taking a bit out of his bagel.

The two doctors ate their breakfast and talked about other patients. Even though Emily was consumed with Lisa she was still treating other patients and had to give her boss updates on them. Although none of them were nearly as interesting as Lisa and none of them were a mirror for how she used to be. Finally when the two were done talking Dr. Carlson pulled out a folder and asked Emily an important question.

"Emily, when did your mother die?"

"My father said she died about four years ago, he read her obituary in the newspaper."

"How did she die?"

"Paper said she committed suicide, we've talked about this before, why are you asking me again?"

"Because I stumbled upon something interesting when reading Lisa's file after we got all the background information back and I wanted to double check something."

Dr. Carlson handed her the file and Lisa's mother's information was highlighted with a date of death. She had committed suicide about four years ago. Emily looked at the date and winced, but she didn't see anything odd. She looked at Dr. Carlson and said.

"I don't get it, her mother died about the same time as mine, but it's just a coincidence."

"Look at her date of birth."

Emily did and it was the same date of birth as her mother. Now she was shocked a little bit, but it still didn't prove anything because it wasn't out of the realm of possibility that their mother's shares the same birthday and had both committed suicide. Dr. Carlson said. "The only reason I recognize the day is because you always go to church and light a candle for your mother on that day...her birthday. It's the only time you ever go to church."

Emily looked at him with a scared look and said. "I know what it looks like, but maybe we're just two people who've both had mothers that committed suicide."

"You may be right. However you are connected to her because of that."

"We share a lot of similarities and we've walked the same road, that's why you wanted me to help her, but I won't believe in a lie. I'm not the patient."

"True, but remember you're eleven years older than Lisa and your mother had more children right after she left you and your father. It's a huge coincidence."

"Even so, I still won't believe in something that may not be true and I can't let it cloud my objectivity with Lisa."

Dr. Carlson smiled at her. Then he said. "Good Girl... I just wanted to make sure you're still with me. If you want me to do some more checking and see if we can find out for sure then I will."

"No." After that she got up and left taking her coffee with her. Emily didn't want to think about it. All she needed to be was the doctor to Lisa, not a sister. But Dr. Carlson was right in a way. Lisa and Emily were connected because of their mothers, they had shared similar fates, but we're connected to every living thing. We are a part of everything, we share all that exists within us and so it leads us to share the same fates, the same tragedies, and the same joyful moment. That's what the Buddha would have you believe. But we always have a choice in the end and that's what makes us different. Our choices make us unique because they're our own personal choices.  And that makes all the difference in the end.


∞ ∞ ∞ ∞ ∞


Lisa was sitting alone as usual during breakfast. Since the day she arrived she never bothered trying to get to know people. The only people she knew outside of Dr. Bennett were Rose and her roommate, Lisa of Earth, and that's because they engaged her in conversation. Some days Rose would come by and talk to her during a meal, but some days she would be left alone. Today Rose decided to pay her a visit and for the first time Lisa had a serious question for her. Rose sat down and asked Lisa.

"How are the meds treating you?"

Lisa laughed at the question, it was an unusual one. The medications that Lisa was on especially since she tried to kill herself didn't react very well with her. She was used to drugs, but instead of getting her high, the medications were making her better - perhaps that's why she felt strange. Lisa replied to Rose.

"The meds are treating me about as well as can be expected, thanks for asking."

"The meds around here are meant to make you forget the demon inside."

"What do you mean?"

Rose came closer to Lisa until their faces were only inches apart. Then she said. "The demon is in all of us. We learn to live because of it, but it puts us in here. The meds try to keep it quiet, but they cannot kill it. Sometimes it has to be released."

Lisa gave her a funny look as Rose went into her usual rant, *1 is infinite possibilities, I'll try, but I won't succeed. It's over now. 1 is infinite possibilities, I'll try, but I won't succeed. It's over now.* Lisa still didn't understand what it meant – maybe it wasn't supposed to mean anything, but then again maybe it was an important clue to her freedom from her prison. At this point Lisa didn't know what she was more confused by, the thing that Rose kept saying over and over or what she said about the demon. But she put the thoughts into the back of her mind and asked Rose her question.

"Rose can you remember anything in your life before you came here?"

"Memories fade over the time. The meds take care of that."

"I realize that, but you must remember something."

"No"

"Nothing?"

"Nothing."

"Are you just repeating everything I say now?"

"Yes."

"Why can't you remember? Has it been too long?"

"Important memories never go away. The demon can't let them because they're supposed to be there."

"Why?"

"Why do you think?"

"I don't know. I have all these memories that I thought I'd forgotten and they keep coming back to me, but I'm not sure I'm supposed to have them."

"Rose pulled her face close to Lisa's again and stared for a moment. It made Lisa uncomfortable so she finally said to Rose. "Okay this is weird, but maybe not for a mental facility. Hit me with whatever profound thing you're going to say."

"The memories are who you are and we are the memories we keep. Good, bad, horrific, and they're supposed to be there whether we want them to be or not. The demon's job is to keep within us what's supposed to be there so that we never lose it…so that we never lose who we really are."

And that was it, that's all she said. As usual she said something confusing and profound, got up and walked away. Hopefully in time would it would make sense. That's what Lisa told herself, she was trying to be the optimist. But this was a mental facility and making sense had nothing to do with it. A healing process doesn't have to make sense, it just has to be.

∞ ∞ ∞ ∞ ∞

It was day seven, only a few sessions were left before a judge would make a determination on whether Lisa needed to stay in the hospital or not. Dr. Bennett was making notes before her next session with Lisa trying to decide on what to talk about next. They had already talked about some major issues, but there was still more to talk about. Dr. Bennett felt like that they had only scratched the surface with all the issues that plagued Lisa. Then she looked over at the painting Jake left her – it was the one Lisa had painted in college. That would be her starting point for this session. A few minutes later the orderly brought Lisa to Dr. Bennett's office. Lisa took her usual seat on the couch, poured herself a glass of water then sat there in silence sipping water until the doctor said something to her. Dr. Bennett said hello and then asked her.

"How are you feeling today?"

"It's another day in the loony bin, not the most exciting thing to happen to me."

"Well you have your sarcasm, that's good. You must be getting better."

"My happy pills are doing the trick."

Dr. Bennett laughed at her comment and said." I wanted to thank for being honest yesterday."

"You pushed me to say it."

"No, you said it because you finally wanted to say it out loud. We're not doing anything to your brain that stops you from making a choice. "

"Whatever doctor."

Dr. Bennett grabbed the painting from behind her desk and walked over to Lisa with it. She propped it up on the coffee table near Lisa so she could get a good look at. The she said.

"I want to talk about this painting."

"Where did you get it?"

"Where do you think?"

"Jake...right?"

"Yes. He seems to have a lot of important stuff from you."

"He has things he should have thrown away when he was angry at me after he left."

"I guess it's good for us that he didn't. Now are you going to tell me about the painting?"

Lisa sighed; she was starting to get angry. She was forced to tell something that she wanted to keep hidden the day before and now they were trying to force her again. It was worse than physical torture; that's what she was thinking. Finally in her anger she lashed at and said.

"Fuck you, why can't we just leave the past alone."

"Because your past is what got you here and apparently it's trying to kill you and the fact that you actually haven't succeeded at suicide tells me that you really don't want to die. If that's the case then help me to help you. Let the truth set you free."

"Why does it matter? It's a sad story and not very interesting."

"Lisa we all have a sad story, but they are never uninteresting. It's the happy stories that get boring...it's like reading a hallmark card over and over. The thing is we can't appreciate happiness without feeling sad and that's what makes an interesting story."

"Is that some weird philosophy which will make me want to tell you my sad story?"

"No, I just thought you needed to hear it. The only reason you should tell me is because it will help you even though you can't see it now."

Lisa sighed and sat back on the couch. She didn't want to keep fighting with the doctor because she knew it would lead to being in restraints again. Lisa didn't like the infirmary before and another fight would certainly lead her to do something that required her to go back. Lisa poured herself another glass of water, took a sip and after a couple of minutes of stalling she said.

"I painted it in college. It's what I thought we all were."

"You mean prisoners."

"Yeah something like that."

"Did you view the world as a prison back then?"

"I thought college was a prison."

"Where you went to college or college itself was a prison."

"Didn't matter at that time it's how I viewed things."

Dr. Bennett sat back in her chair and thought for a moment. She made some notes on her notepad then she asked Lisa.

"When did you paint the painting?"

"I guess it was my junior year in college?"

"Before or after the incident involving your mother?"

"Why does it matter?"

"I want to know and I think it's an important question."

Lisa sat and thought for a moment. She couldn't remember off the top of her head when she painted the piece. Finally she remembered and replied.

"I took an art class the next semester after that incident. I painted it in that class."

"Did you get to pick the assignment or did the professor assign the theme to you."

"I'm pretty sure I picked it. Kind of a weird theme to be assigned by a professor I would think."

Dr. Bennett laughed and she said. "I agree it's kind of weird to be assigned something like that, but you never know in an art class where you're supposed to express yourself."

"I don't know why I kept it, it's a sad painting, but I guess I kept it because it's the best one I ever did."

"Or maybe it's a reminder."

"A reminder of what?"

"I don't know," Dr. Bennett said. "Only you can answer that?"

Lisa had a strange look on her face as if she didn't understand the question. But the truth was, she just didn't want to answer the question – she wasn't ready. She replied to Dr. Bennett.

"I don't see the point in leaving ourselves reminders of the past and if that's what this painting really is then I should have destroyed it years ago."

"That's what's really sad about you?"

"What's that supposed to mean?"

"Lisa we always need reminders of where we've come from so we know we're going. It's easy to forget that past especially when you don't want to face it. But there is something really sad about you when you're willing to throw out something that was obviously important to you Perhaps you need it to remind you of what you used to be."

Lisa didn't know how to respond. She shot Dr. Bennett an angry look. Lisa was mad at her for taking a pleasant conversation and making her feel bad again. But Dr. Bennett wasn't really doing that – she was forcing Lisa to take a cold hard look at herself. Since Lisa was not going to answer the question she decided to end the session on a question that Lisa could sit and ponder for a night. She asked Lisa.

"I just want to ask you one more question and you can think about it over night. Lisa do you really, really want to die because it seems to me that for you living is a waste of time. Think about it."

Lisa gave her an angry look and then tears started to well up in her eyes. Dr. Bennett got up and handed her a tissue paper. Lisa just didn't know how to answer the question- the obvious answer was no, but then again it could be yes. She had thought about that many times, that much she could admit to herself. Dr. Bennett said to her.

"I have found that the hardest question to answer for ourselves is always the simple and direct question. Who we are...what's our purpose in life... do we want to live or to die. But if we can answer those questions then we'll find peace. Something else for you to think about. "

Lisa just stared at her, there was no emotion, but she was thinking about the question and that was something. She was escorted back to her room and then started to write in her journal. Life or Death: it's a hard question to ignore because it seems to sum up our complete existence. If we want to live we find purpose in this life and it

gives us a reason to go on living. If we want
to die then what's the point, we might as
well get on with it and it was that question
that Lisa had been trying to answer since
she was a little girl. Although she couldn't
say it out loud she had been thinking about
that question all of her life. So she wrote in
her journal and somewhere in there she
found an answer.

# DAY 8

Emily sat in her office staring out the window and thinking. This case had been a hard one because it was like looking in the mirror. Emily had been there before. There were a lot of things on her mind because of this case. She thought about Lisa and already knew what it would take for her to leave this place. But would she be able to do it. Emily thought about her father, she actually hadn't spoken to him in over a year. She didn't see the point. Emily didn't want to be reminded of the past anymore than Lisa did. She couldn't find anything to talk about with her father – he was a sad alcoholic that couldn't be happy no matter how much he tried and why would she

want to be around that. As she was
thinking she got an email from Jake.

He still wouldn't come by the hospital
and see Lisa, but he wanted to check up on
her. Also with his email was an attachment.
Jake mentioned in his email that she had
left a journal at his place and he found it in
a box of things that he meant to get back to
her after they broke up, but never did.
There were a couple of pages scanned and
attached to the email. It was two journal
entries she made after her mother died
years before. Emily read them and she
actually shed a few tears, the words were
sad and painful. They were words from a
writer who was crying out for help and they
were probably the most honest words that
Lisa had ever said. Emily read the words
over and over.

*January 19th*

*Well my mother finally died today. I
guess it was only a matter of time. Can't
remember her ever being happy and killing
herself, it's not that big of surprise. Of course
my brother can't admit the truth; he still
thinks that this is an accident and that our
mother could never do that to herself. He
was always good at ignoring the obvious. I
wish I had that kind of talent. I know that I
am supposed to feel sad and maybe I do in*

some small way, but I can't cry for my mother. I don't feel anything. Is that wrong? She never cared about me so why should I care about her death. People say that when your mother dies you feel some great loss that never gets replaced, but I don't feel a loss at all. I don't think she was even my mother, at least that's the way I feel some days, but then I know I'm just like her on so many ways. I can't say any of this out loud, not even to Jake, my boyfriend. He's been great, I've only known him a couple of months and I already know that I could probably spend the rest of my life with him. He could be my best friend, my soul mate, and how he's been there for me over the last week is evidence of that. Nobody has ever been there like that for me. All of this that I am feeling, I may never be able to say out loud, but I have to at least say it here even if it's only for me to read.


*January 24th*


Every day I see how I'm more and more like my mother. I know that I'm her daughter, there's no doubt about it. I wonder if I have her bad qualities as well. I wonder if I have her illness. Is it only a matter of time for me before I'm dead? Will I kill myself too when it gets too hard to keep going?

It was hard for Emily to read the journal entries, maybe because she couldn't find a good answer on why Lisa should keep living. Not a good thing for a doctor trying to help her, but she also knew the honest truth, if she had lived Lisa's life then she might not be able to find a reason to keep living either. And Lisa was right in a way; you might as well get on with it. But her job as a doctor in trying to help people prevented her from accepting that answer.

There was something else in the email as well. Jake said that after the journal entry on January 24th Lisa had a bad car accident that nearly killed her. She ran a red light and according to some witnesses it seemed as though it was intentional. Nobody could say for sure, after all it was just an accident and accidents could never be done on purpose. Jake also said that he always had his suspicions about that accident. There were times when there were together that it seemed Lisa was thinking about death. And for Jake if he had found her dead in the middle of night he wouldn't have been surprised. There were many times that she was unhappy and nobody, not even him, could do anything for her. His last thoughts in the email were things that he had never mentioned before and he figured writing them to a doctor was as good of a person as any to tell those things to. His greatest fear was never that she couldn't love him enough but that he could never love her enough - he was wrong because he loved her more than she ever loved him. Jake also feared that no matter how much he loved her it would never be enough. It turned out that he was right.

∞ ∞ ∞ ∞ ∞

Later that day Dr. Bennett had her session with Lisa. She cancelled the rest of her afternoon so she would have more time with Lisa since it was already day eight and they would have to make a determination about her with a judge in two days. Although they had made progress it still wasn't enough, there were things Lisa wasn't talking about and she needed to. It was time for her to do that today if she was going to be saved so she could leave in ten days. Dr. Bennett already knew that she would have to be firm with Lisa to get the whole truth even if it pushed her over the edge and she was prepared to do that.

Lisa was escorted inside the office. She took a seat in her usual spot on the couch and poured herself a glass of water like she always did at the beginning of session. Dr. Bennett asked how she was doing like she always did and of course Lisa replied that she was doing fine. They got through the pleasantries and then Dr. Bennett jumped right into the sessions, holding nothing back. She said to Lisa.

"Today I want to talk about your suicide attempts."

Lisa replied in anger. "Do you ever listen to me, I keep telling you that I've never tried to commit suicide, I've had a few accidents, but that's it."

"You may not have deliberately tried to kill yourself, but you have tried to get other people to kill you and it's just the same."

"Well you're full of shit."

"Maybe, but we're still going to talk about it and we'll sit here all day until you start telling me the truth."

"Hey if you want to waste time talking about the same stuff we've talked about already then go ahead, but my answers aren't changing."

Dr. Bennett poured herself a cup of coffee and then she looked at Lisa with a serious look. It was firm and it was meant to make Lisa uncomfortable. She just stared at Lisa for a moment until Lisa asked her what she was looking at. Finally she spoke.

"Lisa do you know why I asked that question about wanting to die yesterday?"

"Because you were bored and had nothing else to ask."

"No, I wanted you to try and be honest with yourself and if you could do that then maybe you can start being honest about your suicide attempts."

"You're not going to let this go no matter what I tell you are you?"

"Look, you can deny it all you want, but there are too many witnesses to your last incident that say you provoked to the clerk and urged him to shoot you. And your previous attempts have too much evidence that suggest you were doing it intentionally. Everything points to you trying to commit suicide"

"How many incidents are you referring to?"

"I count three over the last ten years, have there been more."

"No, which incidents are you talking about?"

"There was the one when you were 20 and tried to kill yourself with your pain pills, the car accident a few years ago where you ran a red light after being stopped at it for about 30 seconds, and then the latest one with the clerk that got you here."

Lisa sat back on the couch for a moment to think. She was trying to remember the car accident, she had blocked that incident out of her mind years ago, but now she remembered, although she remembered the whole thing differently. But her real question was how Dr. Bennett found out about. She asked Dr. Bennett that very question.

"How did you find out?"

"An old friend of yours told me."

"It must have been Jake, right?"

"Yes, He gave me some more of your things and told me about the incident since it happened right after your mother died?"

"Can't you see what he's doing?"

"What's that?"

"He's making up stuff about me to get back at me because he got hurt. There's no telling what he'll say about me, but it's all lies."

"You think he's doing this for revenge against a former lover?"

"Of course he is he's no different than any other guy that I must have hurt when we broke up. They always want to get me back for it."

"So you think every guy you've ever dated and broke up with is out to hurt you."

Sure, why wouldn't they want to get me back?"

"Did you ever think that they may not have that big of a grudge against you to waste the time Maybe they just don't want to remember. I think you're making up accusations against Jake because he told me something about your past that you didn't want me to know. "

"That's bullshit."

"Is it, because I think it's easier to blame somebody else for hurting you instead of accepting responsibility for your own actions? What do you say about that, your two famous words?"

Lisa didn't say anything she shot Dr. Bennett a dirty look, same as she always did when she was cornered. She sat back and ignored the doctor. Dr. Bennett put her pen and notepad down to wait out the silent treatment. She was going to force her to say anything, not this time, but she was going to wait all night if she had to until Lisa started talking, until she started telling the truth. There was no time to waste; the moment of truth had come for Lisa even if she didn't want to admit it. And for Dr. Bennett she wasn't going to let it be another session where they quit talking and Lisa goes back to her room and then they would talk tomorrow. Tomorrow was already here.

After about five minutes Lisa decided to speak. Dr. Bennett was brewing another pot of coffee, preparing for a long night. She was going to make sure that when it came to a battle of wills she would win, but Lisa decided to speak. She said.

"The car incident was an accident despite what everybody thinks. Did I have thoughts about killing myself...sure, but I wasn't going to kill myself like that."

"Did you want somebody else to do it for you?"

"No."

"What about when you were 20 and you tool all those pain pills?"

"Why do we have to keep talking about that?"

"Because you haven't told me the truth yet."

"I told you, I didn't realize how many pills I was taking at the time, it was an accident."

"I'm not talking about that. I want to know what you and your mother fought about that made you so angry?"

"Typical mother and daughter stuff?"

"That doesn't make you want to kill yourself, what's the real story?"

"How do you know I'm lying, I never got along with my mother, one fight could have pushed me over the edge. Maybe it was a series of fights that had been building towards something tragic."

"I believe that can be true, but I don't think it's the real story with you."

"You don't want to believe what I tell you because it's not what you want to hear. It's not interesting enough for you is it?"

Dr. Bennett sighed for a moment and then got angry. She lashed out and said. "I want to believe you, but you haven't given me anything to believe yet. Now will you just tell me the fucking truth and quit wasting my time."

"You shouldn't get so angry Dr. Bennett. Wanting something that doesn't really exist is not going to make you happy."

Dr. Bennett got up and put her notepad and pen on her desk. She had enough. Although she was willing to wait all night for answers, she wasn't going to be "dicked" around by Lisa. If Lisa wanted to play games then she could do it in her room on 100 milligrams of Thorezine. Dr. Bennett called the orderlies to come and get Lisa so she could go back to her room. Lisa heard her say that on the phone and got angry. She knocked her glass of water over in anger so that it fell of the table and broke on the floor. She shouted.

"What the hell is wrong with you, I'm cooperating with you."

"No you're not," Dr. Bennett replied. "You screwing me around and if you're going to do that then we're done. The purpose of these sessions is to work with me and try to get better. And you can only do that by telling the truth."

"I am telling you…"

Dr. Bennett stopped her before she could finish the sentence and said. "No you're not because something pretty horrific happened to you that made you want to die and a simple fight with your mother isn't it. It's something else."

"How do you know if that's true?"

"I'm a psychologist, it's my job to know people, especially when they're lying or can't admit something horrible."

A couple of the orderlies and a nurse walked in the office. Lisa froze, she was scared -she was scared of going back into the restraints, which she thought would be the outcome. Dr. Bennett said. "We're done Lisa unless you can finally find the courage to talk about what happened. It has to be pretty bad if you keep repressing those memories and trying to deny what really happened."

Lisa started to cry as the orderlies approached her. Her back was against the wall and she didn't know what to do. So somewhere deep within she found the words and screamed out loud. "It was my stepfather...he raped me."

Dr. Bennett stopped the nurse and the orderlies then motioned for Lisa to take a seat. She told the nurse and orderlies to wait outside until she was done. Then she said to Lisa. "Tell me what happened."

It was hard for Lisa to control herself; her words were mixed with tears. She couldn't even look at Dr. Bennett in the eyes. But Lisa began to tell the story, every detail, every memory that she had repressed.

Lisa had never really like her mother's third husband. He seemed nice, but there was always something about him that could make you feel uncomfortable. She never took the time to really get to know him because she never wanted to. And when Lisa expressed her concerns to her mother of course her mother never

listened to her, she just told Lisa that she
had a depressing imagination. He mother
was blinded by how nice this guy was to
her and by the fact that he had money. It
was the same old story with Lisa's mother
and the ending never changed.

So it happened during the time that
Lisa had broken her foot and couldn't get
around on her own. She was spending a
couple of weeks with her mother and her
second stepdad. For the most part staying
with them was okay and her mother's
husband was extremely nice. Lisa started to
think that maybe she was wrong about
him, but her instincts told her different.
One night when it was just the two of them
at the house he made dinner for her and
gave Lisa her pain medication. The
medication made Lisa very drowsy and all
she was taking was 1 pill 3 times a day.
Because of it she would sleep most of the
day.

Lisa was trying to tell this story
without hesitating or without any tears, but
she couldn't. It was still too hard for her to
say the words out loud, but she found a
way. Her stepdad put a couple pain pills in
her food and then still gave her one pill with
her meal. About 20 minutes later Lisa fell
asleep, but she wasn't completely asleep.
That's when it happened. Her stepdad
moved her around on the couch for better

access and started to take off her clothes. Lisa had big breasts so he started with lifting up her shirt and taking off her bra – he played with her breasts for a couple of minutes. Then he started with the pants. When he took off her pants that's when Lisa started to wake up. She caught him and tried to fight him off, but she wasn't very successful. He was stronger and was able to pin her to the couch with his body weight since he had crawled on top of her. She tried, she really did try and fight; she was too drowsy and not strong enough so she closed her eyes and drifted back into a light sleep hoping that it would be over soon. Fortunately it was and he put her cloths back on trying to act like nothing happened. After that all she tried to do was forget about it especially after she tried to tell her mother what happened and mother wouldn't listen. Lisa with tears in her eyes and her words not making much sense went on to say.

"That night after I spoke to my mother, I took the pain pills to completely forget. I didn't care what they did to me. Death would have been okay with me."

Dr. Bennett walked over to her and said." I can understand why, there are plenty of moments that we don't want to live again. Pills, a needle in the arm, or alcohol can make you forget."

"I wasn't trying to deliberately kill myself, but if you want to know the truth there are times that I don't want to live...being dead would be easier to live with."

"Sometimes death can be that for us. What happened with your mother and that guy?"

Lisa with tears still in her eyes said. "They eventually got a divorce. He was accused of molesting a boy in the Boy Scout troupe he sponsored.

"Did your mother ever believe you about what your stepdad did you after that?"

"No, she always said that it couldn't have happened because I wasn't a little boy. My mother never wanted to believe it."

Dr. Bennett looked at Lisa and put her hand on hers. She said. "You know that it's not your fault, it's just something terrible that happened. We can't control things like that."

"But I could have fought him off; it's my fault because I let it happen."

"No it's not."

"It's always my fault; I let things happen to me."

"No, that's not true."

Lisa began to cry again. She couldn't control her words anymore. Dr. Bennett tried to hold and comfort her. She said to

Lisa. "You don't have to blame yourself for what happened."

"I am to blame," Lisa said. "I always am. My ex-husband was right."

"No, don't talk like that."

"I made my stepdad do that to me."

Dr. Bennett was hugging Lisa now trying to calm her down and telling her over and over that it wasn't her fault. Finally Lisa let out a scream and pushed Dr. Bennett out of the way. She found an open corner of the room and fell to the floor, crying, and screaming out, "I won't let you do this to me." Dr. Bennett didn't know if it was directed towards her or she was finally fighting back against her stepdad through her repressed memories. Dr. Bennett tried to help her, but Lisa pushed her out the way. Finally the orderlies and nurse were ordered back into the office so they could help Lisa to her room. As they were taking Lisa out of the office and walking her down the hall she continued to scream out loud those same words over and over until they were a fading sound in the hospital, "I won't let you do this to me."

# DAY 9

When Emily was working on a hard case she would from time to time wake up to bad memories. Since working with Lisa she was having a lot more than usually. She was remembering things that she thought had been forgotten and with good reason, she had already dealt with those issues before. That's what she told herself, but working with Lisa was like looking in a mirror. More and more memories would come to the surface. On the 9th day since Lisa had been admitted to the hospital Emily woke up remembering one of the darkest times in her life. The only question she had was why.

Emily remembered the day her divorce was final. She was a little sad, but most of all glad that it was finally over. What her ex-husband did was humiliating, but there was still one question she had for him. She hadn't gotten the chance to ask it yet, they had spent too much time fighting over who got what in the divorce. So after the hearing was over and the verdicts had been rendered Emily stopped her ex husband outside the courthouse and asked him.

"I need to ask you something and I need you for once in your life to be completely honest."

"Jesus Emily, we're done and I got places to be."

"You owe me an answer."

"Fine, what do you want to know?"

"Why did you cheat on me, if you didn't want to be with me anymore? Couldn't you have just been honest with me?"

"I don't have an answer for you Emily, I did what I did and you don't have to like it."

"Did you ever love me?"

Her ex-husband stared at her and after a few moments Emily told him to answer the question. He said to her. "I don't think I ever really loved you, at least not enough." And that was it. He walked away leaving her on the steps of the courthouse. Emily never saw him again, but she never forgot his last words to her. He was cruel and the cruelty is what she carried it with her every day.

Then Emily remembered what she did next. She walked until she found a place that could give her something to fix the pain. Emily found a drug dealer standing outside a sub-shop. She bought a bag of pot and a dose of heroin. Emily had smoked pot in college, but she had never had heroin before. The heroin would make her forget all her bad memories for the next year of her life until the person she used to be couldn't be recognized anymore.

Emily put the memory away as she got ready for the day. It was the last day she would have with Lisa before the hearing and there were still things to talk about. But that would have to wait – she had something important to do. It was something that she didn't want to do, but she had to do it anyway. Emily had to visit her father.

Before she went to work she drove out to his place. Her father still lived in their childhood home. The only thing different about the house was that it was more run down, decaying on the outside just like the man who lived inside of it. When she saw it she was shocked, it was not like she remembered. Of course she hadn't been to the house in over ten years. The paint on the outside had faded and was chipping off. The roof looked as if it could cave in at anytime. The house was basically rotting from the inside out.

Emily walked in and found her father preparing breakfast, the house smelled like bacon. Instead of having coffee prepared like most people he had orange juice and a bottle of vodka. She walked into the kitchen and said hi. The old man didn't seem to recognize her and was a little shocked to see a stranger in his house or at least who he thought was a stranger. Emily said to him."

"Dad it's me Emily."

He looked her up and down then paused for moment, trying to convince himself that it was actually true; his daughter was standing in front of him. He was drunk of course, even this early in the morning, but after a few moments the old man knew that it was her. He replied.

"It's been a long time... I thought you would never come back and see me."

"I admit I've thought about many times."

"You probably have every right too. Good to see you, how are you?"

"I'm fine dad."

"Are you married again... have any kids?"

"No, work keeps me pretty busy so I don't have time for that."

"Me neither. I'm too busy for any of that as well."

The old man looked at the bottle of vodka smiling at her trying to make a joke. Emily looked over at the bottle of vodka and rolled her eyes. She changed the subject by asking the old man.

"I need to ask you a question so I need you to remember something. How long ago was it when you heard about mom's death"

"It was about four years ago I guess, why?"

"Something strange happened at work and I wanted to know. Do you know how she died?"

"I read in the paper that it was a suicide. Witnesses said that she jumped in front of a moving bus."

"You told me one time that not too long after she left you that she got married to someone else."

"Yeah I guess that's right. I don't understand why you want to know all of this?"

Emily took a seat at the kitchen table while her dad finished cooking his eggs and bacon. She paused for a moment, trying to stop the tears that were starting to well up in her eyes. The she asked.

"How did you find out about her marrying someone else?"

"It was about 3 months after she walked out-the day we signed the divorce papers she was with that other guy and they were getting married at the courthouse after everything was finalized with our divorce. She apparently met him the month before. She was also pregnant at the time so I guess they were having to get married in a hurry."

"She was pregnant, how did you know that?"

"Your mom was showing and getting pretty big."

Emily paused for a moment to think about all of it. Something was not right. Her dad had to be off with his time frame. She asked him if he was sure about what he said, after all he was a drunk, but he said he was sure. Then he asked again why she asking him these questions. Emily said to the old man.

"If mom was showing when you saw her three months later that means she was about 5 or 6 months pregnant. That also means that the guy she married couldn't have been the father. She was already pregnant. Chances are the baby she had was yours."

The old man looked at her with no emotion on his face. He just went back to cooking his breakfast and then poured himself another screwdriver. Emily looked at him strangely, she couldn't believe that even after all these years he didn't care. So she asked him.

"Dad don't you even care?"

"No."

"Why not?"

"It has nothing to me. Don't know for sure if what you're saying is true. Your mother left 30 years ago and I stopped caring when she walked out that door."

"No you stopped caring a long time before that, that's why she left."

The old man slammed the spatula on the corner and turned around in anger facing Emily. He said to her. "You're mother was a selfish bitch, who didn't care about anybody but herself. She wasn't a good wife. She couldn't please a man. She wasn't even a good mother…she never loved you. I hated being around her and that's why I never came home…it was always better being away from her. It was a good thing she left because I would have thrown her out, anyway"

Emily had tears in her eyes. She was hoping to find a decent man still left inside her father, but he drank that away a long time ago. She needed the truth about her mother that day and although she found out some details it only helped to confirm her suspicions about the other life her mother lived. And all Emily could find at home was a bitter old man whose life seemed to be inside a bottle of vodka. His angry rants about who her mother really was, was evidence of that. She looked at her father and said.

"I was hoping that after all these years I could come home and find something good in you, but I guess you never had it at all. You're a sad pathetic soul, maybe you're the one who should have left 30 years ago instead of driving my mother away."

The old man looked at her with rage in his eyes. He threw his glass of orange juice and vodka across the room. Emily got startled at the sound of crashing glass against the kitchen wall. He grabbed his daughter by the arm and shoved her through the kitchen door into the driveway. Then he said.

"Get the hell out of here you fucking bitch. I don't ever want to see you again."

He slammed the door and she slowly walked down the driveway looking through the windows of the kitchen trying to see her dad. Emily suddenly felt like that 6 year old little girl again needing her daddy to make everything alright just like he used to before he started drinking and became the miserable person he was now. She tried to remember how he really was back then, but the only memory she had left of him was a drunken father who yelled at her all the time and an old man who slammed the door in the face of his only daughter. Emily drove away and that would be the last time she ever saw her father again until she got a call from the police a few years later because she was the next of kin, he was found dead. He had died of alcohol poisoning.

∞ ∞ ∞ ∞ ∞

It was already later in the day when Dr. Bennett looked at her watch and noticed that it was time for her session with Lisa. It was the last one before her hearing and there was only one thing that Lisa needed to do to set herself free. It's what we all have to do when we've hit rock bottom and have to crawl our way back up. Instead of having the session in her office Dr. Bennett decided to have it in Lisa's room. She figured Lisa had gone back and forth enough so Dr. Bennett walked out of her office and walked down the long hallway past the dirty white walls that never seemed to be clean. They just lingered there as a reminder of what the hospital really was, a broken down facility with depressed and forgotten people. But there were doctors like her trying to help those that could not help themselves.

Dr. Bennett found Lisa's room and there she was lying on the bed scribbling in her journal. Lisa's roommate was away so they had the room to themselves. Dr. Bennett said hi and asked her how she was doing. Lisa said she was doing fine. Then Dr. Bennett handed her a glass of water. Lisa said thank and then asked her.

"Aren't you forgetting my medication?"

"No medication for you today."

"Am I getting a reward?"

Dr. Bennett laughed and replied to her. "No, it has nothing to do with that. I just came to the conclusion that you don't really don't need it."

"Oh, I thought I was sick."

"Maybe a little bit, but we all are to a degree. However you're not insane."

"So there's nothing wrong with me, is that what you're trying to say?"

"That's not what I am saying. You do have something wrong with you, you have pain and you have anger. And you are depressed, but it's not the kind that can be cured with drugs. You're depression comes from being hurt, it comes from having to live with a pain that you can't let go of until you don't know whether to be a victim or just to give up and die."

Lisa gave Dr. Bennett a shocking look. She didn't understand. If she wasn't insane or didn't need any kind of medication then why was she there? But that shock turned to anger, all she could see what Dr. Bennett judging her and looking down at her for being that way. She asked Dr. Bennett.

"If I'm not really sick or I'm not really like any of the people that are in this place then why do you still keep me here?"

"Because you do need help just like we all do and despite everything you've revealed to me this week, despite all the truth you've finally admitted there is still one thing you haven't done."

"What's that?"

Dr. Bennett looked at her and gave her a smile. "You haven't found acceptance and it's the one thing we always have to do in order to get past the pain…to find healing. We have to accept who we and how we got here despite whether it's our fault or not. It's only through acceptance that we can move on with our life."

"I know who I am and I know what was done to me."

"But can you accept that none of it was your fault and live the rest of your life knowing that bad things happen to us even though it's not our fault and that we still have a choice on how we want to live. I've said it before we can let those bad things destroy us or we can find away to get past them."

Lisa looked away. She turned around from facing Dr. Bennett and stared off at the wall opposite of her and the doctor. Then she said. "It's easy for someone to say all those things, but how can you really know if you've never lived it."

"You think that I walked in your shoes before."

"I think you're just a doctor trying to connect with a patient even if means lying."

Dr. Bennett laughed to herself and then paused for moment. She wanted to show Lisa that she wasn't some doctor, but that she had a tragic story too. Although she had made references to some of the tragic events in her life, she had never told Lisa the whole truth. So to help Lisa understand she did.  She said to Lisa.

"I'm an alcoholic and drug addict."

Lisa laughed. "You've probably never tried any of it in your life so you didn't have to risk losing control."

"I tried heroin for the first time the day my divorce was final. Shot it up in my arm and everything and I've got the scars to prove it." Dr. Bennett showed her the needle marks on her arm. They were still dark and could plainly be seen – they had never healed right even though she had

been clean for almost four years. Lisa saw
them and was surprised. She could see that
the scars were real; she knew it because
she had been addict at one time.  Lisa
asked her as she rubbed the old needle
mark scar on her left arm.

"Why did you start using?"

"Because I wanted to forget. My ex-
husband on the day that our divorce was
final told me that he never really loved me
and I saw him as just another person who
walked out on me. He was just like my
mother – she left me and my dad when I
was eleven. She left on my birthday."

"How did you get clean? Did you even
get clean?"

"Yeah I finally got clean; it was about
a year and a half later. I had to go to rehab.
I nearly lost my medical license. And getting
clean was the hardest thing I ever had to
do. Everything that I tell patients to get
them better like the stages of grief or how to
find acceptant I actually had to learn for
myself. I never did before because it was
just something I read out of textbook and
applied to my patients. But it's a lot
different when you're the patient." Dr.
Bennett had tears starting to well up in her
eyes as she remembered those dark
moments in her life. She remembered the
time she didn't have any money for heroin
and she let two guys screw her at the same

time to score her fix, one guy in front and one guy screwing her from behind. It was painful to remember, but Lisa needed to understand. She needed to understand that she was not alone. Sometimes our story is the story of others for we're all connected in some way.

Lisa sat down and faced Dr. Bennett. She asked her. "How did you live without your mother?"

"It was hard. My father didn't know how to raise me. He was already an alcoholic back then. Most nights I would put him to bed after he passed out in his chair watching TV. When my mother left I didn't have a parent who cared enough to raise me. I basically raised myself. So when I left for college I left for good never going back. Kind of like you."

Lisa gave her a half smile to acknowledge that she was starting to understand. She asked the doctor. "Did you have trouble in relationships growing up?"

"Of course...I never thought anybody could love me because no one did while growing up. Then I made one of the biggest mistakes in my life. I married the first man who ever paid attention to me and told me that he loved me. After that I ignored who he really was because I wanted to feel loved by somebody. I wanted to feel safe. It sounds like a cliché doesn't it?"

"Yes is does...you are your own soap opera.'

"I guess I am," Dr. Bennett said while wiping the tears in her eyes. "But that's my story... it's not an uncommon one, but it's one filled with pain and depression."

"I know the feeling."

Dr. Bennett smiled this time as she said. "I know you do and to tell you the truth when I see you, it's like looking in a mirror. So when I tell you that I've been where you are, it's not just something this doctor will say to try and connect with you."

Lisa had a few tears in her eyes. She was sad because she misjudged the doctor and for the first time realized that her story wasn't that unique, the only unique thing about it was the ending that she could find in this depressing saga. Lisa wasn't in denial anymore, at least right now she wasn't. She looked at Dr. Bennett with the most heartfelt of looks that she had given her since their first session. She asked.

"How did you finally get cured?"

"You don't get cured. I will always be an alcoholic and drug addict. The only difference now is that I don't let the temptation take control. I can ignore it and live with this disease."

"How do you live with it?"

"I live it with it one day at a time. I get up and breath and I start a new day by finding something positive in my life, some kind of purpose that makes my life worth it so I don't do those things anymore. That's also why I am a doctor because I can help other people and that gives me purpose."

"That's it- you just take a deep breath and live out your day ignoring the temptations?"

"It's more than just that. I find acceptance in who I am, and what I used to be. And you know even though it's another cliché I find comfort in the serenity prayer – I'll even pray it at least once a day even though I think it's hard to believe in God, but the prayer gives me comfort."

Lisa looked confused; she didn't know what the prayer was. Of course she had heard it before just like we all have at one time, but she didn't recognize it. Dr. Bennett decided to say it out loud.

*God grant me the serenity to accept the
things I cannot change;
courage to change the things I can; and
wisdom to know the difference.
Living one day at a time;
Enjoying one moment at a time;
Accepting hardships as the pathway to
peace;
Taking, as He did, this sinful world as it is,
not as I would have it;*

Dr. Bennett looked at Lisa after she was done and said. "You see one of the reasons I like this prayer is because it's about finding acceptant within ourselves. That's what I was trying to tell you, you haven't found that yet. That's what's wrong with you and medication isn't going to help you with that."

"But saying this prayer will cure me?"

Dr. Bennett smiled and said to Lisa. "The only power this prayer really has is if we choose to believe it and live by it. Other than that it's just words. The prayer can help you, but you have to believe it and when you can do that then you can find acceptance."

"It's got to be harder than saying a few words and believing in them."

"It is. You have to do it every day. You have to find meaning in your life everyday that helps you get past the pain. Sometimes you have to convince yourself when you get up that it's worth it to keep going. I do that sometimes, even now." Dr. Bennett got up and sat next to Lisa on the bed. She put her hands on Lisa's hands and said. "If you can admit that it's not your fault that you let all these things in your life beat you down and that caused to try and commit suicide, to do drugs then you find acceptance and that will set you free from this place...and from the prison you created for yourself. My recommendation at the hearing is if you can do that then we should let you go."

"If I can admit all that you will let me go?"

"You already admitted it to me this week and if you think that you did it because I pushed you then keep in mind that you still had a choice on whether to tell the truth. You told the truth. But yes if you can do that you will walk out of here."

"And I'll be fine or healed or whatever you call it?"

Dr. Bennett laughed a little bit at the question because Lisa was really searching for a simple answer even though there are no such things. There are only simple questions. She wished that she could say that simple answer, but it would be a lie. Dr. Bennett did say.

"You may never be completely healed. You will have to live with this all of your life, but you can find a way to live your life so that all those tragic events you've been through don't affect it. You can still find a way to be happy. And of course I do recommend that you see a psychologist for awhile so you can talk things out.”

Lisa looked at Dr. Bennett with a sorrowful look and asked her. “What if I can’t do any of what you’ve said? What happens then?”

“You already know the answer to that Lisa. But don’t forget it’s always about acceptance. That’s the key to our prison.”

Dr. Bennett said goodbye and walked out of the room. Lisa just sat on the bed pondering what they had talked about. And she thought about it for the rest of the day, ignoring her roommate and everything around her. She was trying to find her answer - she was trying to find her acceptance.

# DAY 10

For the first time all week Emily got a restful sleep. She didn't wake up to bad memories. She felt at peace like the weight of the world had been lifted off her shoulders. And for the first time all week she went to work with a smile. She arrived a little early and saw her boss for their usual breakfast meeting. He asked her about Lisa since there was a hearing about her in two hours.

Emily said. "I think she'll be fine."

"You think that she'll tell the truth in the hearing," Dr. Carlson asked, "the same truth that she told you this week."

"Well I hope she told me everything, but if you want to know what I think she'll say in there then yeah I think she'll admit what her problem is."

"Okay, we'll see."

"You don't think that she will?"

"I don't know, I've seen a lot of strange things in a hearing like this.

Sometimes patients aren't as ready as we think they are. But that doesn't mean you haven't done a good job with her. You did what most doctors couldn't do."

"Considering everything I've been through."

"That's right. You can't tell me that helping her wasn't like looking at yourself a few years ago. But I also know that there wasn't any other doctor around her that could do it."

Emily smiled at her boss. It felt good to have someone believe in her and he never lost faith in her. Even when she went through the darkest days in her life with alcohol and drug addiction he was always there for her believing that she could be better than what she was. He was the main reason she got and was able to keep her medical license. Truth be told, he was more of father to her than her real one. He was what a parent should be – the first person you call because they never let you down and they never lose faith in you.  Emily and Dr. Carlson finished their breakfast and talked about Emily's other cases.  Then she left and got ready for the hearing.

∞ ∞ ∞ ∞ ∞

While Dr. Bennett was having breakfast with her boss Lisa got an unexpected visitor. It was the police officer who arrested her and brought her to the hospital. It was strange that she was allowed in the bedroom and didn't have to wait in the visitor's area. Then again she was a police officer, perhaps she could do that. She wanted to check on Lisa before the hearing. Lisa thought it was strange, but she was glad for the company because she wouldn't see anybody until the hearing and she knew that it would be uncomfortable. Officer Reyes asked her.

"So how are you doing?"

"Fine I guess."

"This place isn't treating you too bad I hope."

"I've been in worst places. My only complaint is that they don't clean the walls around here."

"Officer Reyes laughed and replied to her. "Yeah they should get on that."

"So what are you really doing here Officer?"

"I just wanted to tell you before you go into the hearing not to forget."

"Not to forget what?"

"Don't forget what you used to be. You weren't always miserable - there was a time when you were happy and full of life."

"I can't remember when that was."

Officer Reyes smiled and said. "You should try. It would be unfortunate to become someone that you don't want to be."

"Hopefully that won't happen." Lisa said as she smiled at Officer Reyes.

"But it does happen when we least expect it. That's why I wanted to come by and tell you before you have you're hearing. Take a good look and see what you used to be because you can still be that again.

"Thank you... I think."

"Take care Lisa, one way or another your life will change today...for good or for the worse."

And that was it. Office Reyes shook Lisa's hand and walked out. It was a strange conversation, but the truth is Lisa needed the reminder. No matter how difficult and no matter how much she wanted to forget Lisa needed to see what she used to be.

∞ ∞ ∞ ∞ ∞

Later that day Lisa was escorted to the conference room of the hospital where the hearing with the judge would take place. The orderlies sat her outside the room and waited with her until it was time to go in. As she sat down she looked down the long hallway surrounded by dirty white walls, that's when she saw someone that she had not seen in a long time. It was Jake and he was walking down the hallway with a nurse towards the conference room. Lisa was shocked because she thought that she would never see him again after he walked out on her eight months ago.

Jake looked at her when he got to the conference room and said hi, but that was all. Lisa still stunned didn't say anything. Finally after about 60 seconds she asked Jake. "What are you doing here? I thought you didn't want to see me again."

"I still don't," He said. "But your doctor asked me to be a character witness on your behalf and I wasn't going to let my hatred stop me from doing something nice for you."

"If you're going to tell them what a horrible person I am and that I need to be in here then I would prefer that you wouldn't say anything at all."

"Even after all this time you still underestimate me. Just because I don't like you doesn't mean that I'm here to sabotage you. I don't want to see you in this place. I want you to get help. Maybe this place was good for you the last ten days, but you don't need to be locked away here either. You're a better person being out of a place like this. You're good at your job no matter how messed up you are emotionally or mentally – you should be out there doing it."

"I didn't mean to suggest that you were..."

Jake cut her off before she could finish her sentence and he said to her. "You never mean to suggest anything bad about me, but you do. You never wanted to see how much I loved you or how good I could be in your life. I guess I was too foolish to think that you could.  You always saw the worst in me even when it wasn't true, but I see the best in you and that's what I hope you can be again. "

Lisa smiled and said to Jake. "Thank you; you're a good man Jake. You were always good to me."

"I know and whether you want to believe it or not I still care about you. That's why I'm here."

Lisa smiled again and tears started to well up in her eyes. She felt happy and saddened that she had pushed Jake away. But while she felt that way she also felt angry. She was still angry at Jake for blaming her. After all she had been honest with him and he wouldn't accept her answer on one what kind of relationship she wanted from him. And that happiness she felt turned to fear because she still felt like Jake would say something bad and paint her as someone completely vindictive and crazy. Her emotions mixed with her anger and her pain were like a rollercoaster ride – that was a dangerous thing before going into a hearing that could determine whether she could be set free or not.

A few minutes later the Lisa was brought into the conference room. The hearing was informal. The judge sat at the head of a conference table with Lisa, Dr. Bennett, Dr. Carlson, and a court reporter to record everything for public record. The Judge asked Lisa if she understood why she was there and what the hearing was about. Lisa said that she did. The judge asked her if she aware of her rights, such as she could have a lawyer present if she wanted. Lisa said that she understood. The judge explained that he would be asking her questions after he heard testimony from her doctor and any character witnesses. He asked Lisa if she understood this as well. Lisa nodded yes.

Dr. Bennett went first. She gave her report on Lisa and explained everything that they had talked about over the last ten days. Dr. Bennett said her conclusion was that Lisa was not crazy, she didn't suffer from any kind schizophrenia, and that her being suicidal was not really a major concern. While she may have had attempts at suicide she was better now and there was no major concern anymore that she would kill herself if she were to leave the hospital. Lisa didn't have to be locked away under suicide watch. The judge asked her about the incident a few days before where she cut her wrists and had to spend the night in the infirmary. Dr. Bennett explained that she did it out of anger because she did not want to talk about what really happened in her life that caused her to be depressed, but eventually Lisa did talk about it.

Dr. Bennett was really fighting for her and explained to the judge that patients will sometimes do things to themselves out of anger because they don't want to talk; that it doesn't mean that they're insane or suicidal. It's not any more serious than when we get angry and bang our fist against the wall. Lisa had shown a lot of progress over the last ten days and they were able to get at the truth about her life even to the point that she was starting to accept what had happened in her past and that it was not her fault. It was also Dr. Bennett's conclusion that although Lisa might be depressed, she did not need medication or to be locked away. She need to face her demons, deal with her problems, and through outside counseling learn to find happiness in her life again.

The Judge asked Dr. Carlson as head of the medical staff if he agreed with this assessment. He told the Judge that he did. After reviewing the case file the judge

admitted that he was little concerned, but
also admitted that he was not an expert in
mental illness nor had he ever been faced
the things that this patient had been faced
with. He was relying on the expert opinion
of the doctors at the hospital. Then the
judge asked Jake to come forward and have
a seat at the table. As a former friend they
needed to someone to act as a character
witness. So he was asked in his honest
opinion if he thought Lisa was sick and
needed to be in a mental facility. He told
the judge that in his opinion she did not
need to be there. Jake also went on to say
that her problems were not any different or
any more severe than any of one of them in
the room. Of course people get depressed
and feel like their life should end, Lisa was
not any different.

  The judge asked him what he thought
of Lisa. He was honest- she could be
annoying and hard to be with, but she was
a good and kind person. Jake also said that
she was a strong person and he was
amazed how she handled herself, if he had
been through what she had been through
he couldn't say for sure if he wouldn't be in
a mental hospital himself. Lisa however was
able to cope and function in life. He looked
at her when he said that last part. That
part was a bit of a stretch, but he wanted to
prove to Lisa that he was there to help her.

Lisa smiled at Jake when he said that last part. The judge thanked Jake and excused him from the table. Now he wanted to ask Lisa questions.

He looked at Lisa who was getting a glass of water from the pitcher of water on the table. The judge asked if she was ready and if she would tell the whole truth and nothing but the truth.  She agreed. Then the judge asked his first question.

"Lisa, do you believe that you were trying to commit suicide 10 days ago by getting the store clerk to shoot you?"

"No I was not committing suicide. In fact I am not suicidal as these doctors would have you to believe."

Dr. Carlson and Dr. Bennett both looked up at her in shock. They couldn't believe what Lisa was saying so Dr. Bennett interrupted and asked Lisa. "What are you saying... you admitted the truth the day before?"

The judge looked at Dr. Bennett and replied. "Please do not interrupt doctor. Lisa is the only one allowed to speak right now. You had your chance earlier." He looked at Lisa and started asking questions again.

"Lisa, do you believe that you are depressed as Dr. Bennett suggested in her report?"

"No I am not depressed, I'm angry."

"What are you angry at?"

"That these people here keep saying that I have a problem and are making up lies about me. I'm angry at the people that keep trying to hurt me like that man over there."   She pointed at Jake who was caught by surprise by what she was saying. He wanted to believe so much that she was getting better and for once wouldn't blame him for what happened between them. Apparently he was wrong.

The judge asked her. "So you think the problems the doctor said you have are false?"

"Yes they are your honor. I have problems just like everybody else, but not what she's suggesting." Lisa was now looking over at Dr. Bennett with an angry look. The doctor just had a surprised look on her face. Lisa was acting the same way she did on her first day at the hospital. The judge continued.

"Lisa it says here in this report that your mother committed suicide and you were really affected by it, so much so that you tried to commit suicide again by having a car accident. Is this true?"

"I did have a car accident after my mother died, yes, but I was not trying to kill myself. My mother did commit suicide, but I didn't care. I was not that close to my mother and her death didn't mean anything to me."

"There are some journal entries in this file from four years ago that suggest differently." The judge showed her the copies. Lisa looked at them and read the entries. The Judge asked her. "Are those entries true about how you really felt?"

"No, I made it up because my boyfriend at the time was reading my journal trying find out more about me instead of asking me himself, He like to snoop into my personal belongings." She looked at Jake as she said this. "I gave him false answers in the journal because he was looking for someone to rescue and I figured if he saw that in me he would stick around. I know it's pathetic, but I needed a man at the time and I wanted him to stick around. I wanted him to feel sorry for me."

Jake gave Lisa an angry look. She was basically saying that she used him and although he had always had that suspicion about her he still wanted to believe that they had some kind of emotional connection- that they both truly cared for each other."

The judge made his notes and then asked Lisa another question. "Lisa you said this week that your stepfather drugged you and raped you when you were 20 years old. Is that true?"

"No, I just said that because the doctor wanted to hear something tragic about me."

"Why would you do that?"

"Because she kept pushing me to talk about things that were none of her business. She wanted me to tell her how I was tragic and that's why I was suicidal. The doctor made up her own mind about me on the first day and when I didn't measure up to the kind of patient she was looking for she pushed me, trying to get me to admit to stuff that wasn't true. She was looking for a specific kind of patient to save. At this point I would like to make a complaint about her."

The judge rolled his eyes at Lisa and told her that this was not the place to make a complaint. Dr. Bennett started to speak, but the judge motioned for her to stop. Finally she asked the judge if she could ask Lisa a question, it was important. He agreed to it so Dr. Bennett asked Lisa.

"Why are you doing this Lisa? You made progress this week and you were able to deal with the truth. Why act like none of its true. You're taking too many steps back when it comes to acceptance."

Lisa looked at Dr. Bennett and answered the question. "It's not about your version of acceptance. You see me as some troubled girl who doesn't have the right to be angry. You see me as some suicidal maniac who tries to get other people to commit murder because I can't kill myself. You want me to be a victim who ignores everything that's happened to me and needs help from other people. You want me to forgive those that have harmed me and not hold them accountable for their actions. At the end of the day you see me as some poor pathetic girl who can't make it on her own without the help of someone like you. Well I'm none of those things and I won't let you try and make me into them to help you feel better about yourself because you've had a few tough years since your husband left you."

"I've never said that you were any of things," Dr. Bennett said to Lisa. "All I wanted and it's what I want for any patient – for you to find acceptance in the things that happen to you. You don't have to like what happens, but you can't move on without acceptance. You can be angry, it's okay, but you also have to hold yourself accountable for your actions when bad things happen to you and how you can hurt other people when you're angry for what happened to you. You don't have a right to hurt someone else just because you got hurt. I just want you to understand that. That also has something do with acceptance just like we talked about yesterday."

Lisa gave Dr. Bennett an angry look and said. "You only want me the way YOU want me."

"You don't have to do this."

"I have to tell the truth."

Before Dr. Bennett could say anything else the judge interrupted the conversation and said. "You two can argue all you want, but we do have a hearing to conclude and I have a few more questions." He looked at Lisa and asked her.

"Okay Lisa, do you deserve the bad things that happen to you."

"No, but I'm bad luck because bad things always happen to me."

"Do you want to see the people who harmed you punished?"

"I think that they should have something bad happen to them so they know what it feels like."

Jake looked at her in disgust. He felt like in some way that she was directing that comment towards him because he walked out on her even though she had never cared about him or tried to help him in any way. But as he had pointed out so many times before why would anybody stay in a relationship like that. He had every right to leave, but she would never see it that way. In her eyes, he abandoned her.

The judge looked at Lisa and said. "I have one more question. Do you think you belong here?"

"Not because I'm crazy, but it is a lot safer in here because out there is a whole world waiting to harm you...waiting to fuck you over in some way."

The Judge gave Lisa a scolding look for the curse word and then instructed the court reporter to strike it from the record. He told everybody that he had heard enough and was ready to make a ruling but he wanted to offer the doctors or Lisa a chance to add anything. The doctors said they did, they we're still surprised by what Lisa had said, but then they would get a bigger shock. Lisa wanted to say something else. The judge allowed her to and she said.

"I know that the doctor and my friend Jake have a different view of me, but I think I should set the record straight. I am a victim, but I'm not helpless or suicidal. I don't deserve what's happened to me in my past. And I don't think that anybody has ever cared about me, especially those that told me they loved me. I won't accept that I'm some sort of pathetic person who needs help. I certainly won't be bullied into becoming something that someone wants me to be or be the victim for someone to rescue who can't save themselves  If you need to know who I really am ask Officer

Reyes, the woman who brought me here –
she visited me this morning. You can also
ask Rose, an older patient here who knows
me. They should be character witnesses for
me."

Dr. Bennett and Dr. Carlson looked
confused because they didn't know who she
was talking about. The judge asked the
doctors about the people she mentioned.
Dr. Bennett said that they didn't exist.
There wasn't a patient there named Rose in
the hospital. Lisa tried to give a description
of Rose so they could find her. She had long
black hair, big brown eyes, a funny smile,
and medium breasts and that she looked to
be about 50 years old because she had
wrinkles under her eyes. Dr. Bennett said
to Lisa.

"Lisa, that's a description of you
except for the part of being older."

That's not true," Lisa said. "Rose may
look like me, but it's not me."

"I'm not saying it is, but it's a little
peculiar that you would describe yourself
about 20 years older."

"Well about Officer Reyes, she was
real."

"Yes she is," Dr. Bennett said looking
at the judge. "You're Officer Reyes,
remember. You're a police officer. The
woman who brought you to the hospital is
named Officer Jennings.

Lisa got mad and knocked the pitcher of water off the table splashing water on the judge and the doctors.  She shouted that nobody knew what they were talking about. As the orderlies grabbed Lisa and restrained her, the judge asked Lisa.

"Lisa, do you want to stay here at the hospital?"

"I don't want to be in a place where the people I see don't exist and it's in their world." She pointed at Dr. Bennett and Dr. Carlson. "I need a place where I'm safe."

The Judge asked Lisa. "Can you admit the people you've been talking to aren't real?"

"They may not be real for you, but they're real."

The Judge ordered that Lisa be taken back to her room. She was too disruptive. When Lisa heard that she punched one of the orderlies and they had to pin her down and give her a sedative to knock her out. Lisa was carried out of the room down the hallway of dirty white walls. She was still a little bit awake as they carried her down the hall so all she saw as she looked up was a blur of brownish white light on the ceiling before she passed out.

The Judge gave his ruling. Lisa would be committed for six months and then be reevaluated after that. He said that she was obviously disturbed - what she said to Dr.

Bennett over the last few days must have been a lie or if it wasn't she wasn't ready to admit the truth now. Either way, Dr. Bennett's assessment of her was wrong and Lisa needed to be at the hospital for awhile. The Judge who had known Dr. Bennett for a few years now said to her that she may not have been entirely wrong, but she underestimated her patient, it happens, but Lisa did need help. The judge thanked Jake for coming. He signed the necessary paperwork that would have Lisa committed for six months and then left.  Dr. Bennett and Dr. Carlson were completely bewildered by what had happened, but it just goes to show that when a person is filled with a lot of pain and rage you never know what's going to happen at any given moment. There is a time bomb waiting to go off. And Lisa certainly was that, she wasn't ready to face her demons yet. Admitting that we have personal demons doesn't mean we can defeat the beast inside of us – we still have to fight it, sometimes every day.


∞ ∞ ∞ ∞ ∞


Later that day Emily went to Lisa's room to check on her. She was still sleeping from the sedative they gave her earlier. Emily just stared through the window on the door at Lisa. She was still in shock by what happened during the hearing.  George Carlson walked up behind Emily to check up on her. That day was a bad one and he figured she might be an emotional wreck after seeing what happened with Lisa. He also knew that he would find her outside Lisa's room. He asked her.

"How are you holding up kid?"

"Still in shock over what happened."

"And you'll probably be that way for awhile, but what happened isn't your fault."

"I don't blame myself, but I do feel like I failed her." Emily said with regretful tone.

"You did everything you could and if you had screwed up at all this week I would have been there to help you fix it. But you did everything right and you got her talking. I don't think anybody has ever been able to do that before in her life."

Emily looked at her boss with a sad look. She replied. "It still wasn't enough and maybe there was..."

George cut her off before she could finish the sentence and said. "Maybe there was something else you could have done, that's what you think, right.  Emily there's always what ifs and that's the beauty of hindsight, but it can't help you in this situation except to feel miserable. But here's the thing and you already know this

– you can't force someone to help themselves. All you can do is try to help that person to help themselves. You did that with Lisa."

"Maybe you're right, but I'm still going to feel like shit for a while."

"I know because you have a connection with her. But keep in mind that no matter how much you two are alike and how similar the tragic events in your lives have been she's not you and you're not her."

"I know that, but I can still help her." Emily had that same sad look while staring at her boss and then George said something else to her.

"True and you will help over time, but you can't make her solve whatever problems she has. That's up to her."

Emily turned away from George and continued to look at Lisa through the window. Even though she was feeling sad she knew George was right. All she could do was try and help Lisa, but in the end Lisa still had learn to get past her own issues with depression and resentment -with her pain and deep seeded anger. George asked her.

"So who do you think the people are she claims to be seeing or do you think that they're made up?"

"I have a theory about that, "Emily replied. "I think that she's seeing herself; one person is who she used to be and the other one is the person she'll be in about 20 years. Lisa is seeing reflections of herself, kind of an extraordinary thing if you ask me."

George smile at her. She was right it was kind of remarkable to see that in one's self. He replied back. "I think you're right about what Lisa sees and if we do our jobs then perhaps we can help her to see only one person, the person that she is supposed to be today and a happy person at that."

"Hopefully we can be good at our jobs for her sake." Emily said as she smiled

"I also have some other information for you." George pulled out an envelope out of his jacket pocket. "I found out more information on her mother, it's pretty interesting and you should have a look at."

"I told you that I didn't want to know…wish you wouldn't have got any more information on her mother."

"Emily I know what you said, but one day you'll want to know. I'll have the information in my desk for when that day comes and you want to know the truth."

"Emily smiled at him and put her hand on his arm. She said. "I don't think it matters, it won't change anything."

"Maybe not today or tomorrow, but one day it will. You'll have to find out eventually and that's why I ignored your request and got the information anyway. But there is something else you should know about Lisa.  We just got the information back to day." He handed Emily a piece of paper – it was a hospital adoption record. "Lisa had a baby two and a half months ago and she gave it up for adoption. It was a little girl."

Emily was surprised by the news. It meant that she was pregnant at the time her and Jake broke up. The child could be his and he probably didn't know about it. Emily said that out loud to George. He agreed with her assessment. Then she smiled and said.

"You know we look at her as some tragic person who really doesn't care about anybody, but maybe she did do a decent thing. Perhaps she thought that she would end up doing the same thing to that child that her mother did to her. So to protect the child she gave it a fighting chance. She gave the baby up for adoption so that a loving family could have it and raise the child right "

George smiled at her and said. "Maybe you're right." Then he turned and walked away. Emily looked at Lisa and smiled because in some strange way she found hope. She had hope that Lisa could be set free, even though it wouldn't be today. Perhaps one day she would break free from the prison she had created for herself. And that's when she saw it. Lisa's journal was open on the foot of her bed. Emily couldn't see everything in the journal, but she did see in big bold letters on the open page –"ITS NOT OVER. I'M STILL ALIVE." Then Emily saw more words on the next page. Lisa had been writing in her journal.  Maybe she was finding her answers through the words on the pages in the journal. Right now the words were the only true thing she had - they were her honest reflections of the person she used to be and the person that she could be again.

∞ ∞ ∞ ∞ ∞

As Emily was leaving she saw Jake in the parking lot of the hospital. He was waiting for her. Jake needed to ask a question. Emily stopped and talked to him for a moment.

Jake asked her. "Do you think that she will ever leave this place?"

"Yes I do, but it will probably take a long time. I have to believe that even though today was a shocker and a major setback. Are you concerned for her?"

"I always have been doctor even when I was angry and hated her. I just want to know that she's going to be okay."

Emily smiled at him. There was a hope in Jake as well. He was finding forgiveness. She replied. "It's good that you feel that way. You should visit her from time to time so she knows that someone still cares for her."

Jake smiled at her and said. "Thank you for saying that. I don't know if you know this, but Lisa put herself through college working as a stripper and it was a club that was fully nude. The ladies at the club did other things as well if you know what I mean. Not many people know she did that. She told me one time that it was the only way she could make money for school because men only saw her as a sex object. And if that's the only way men were going to look at her then she should make money from it."

Emily with a sad look on her face said. "I'm not surprised after hearing everything she's been through. But I'll tell you this. It's one more reason you should visit her. Lisa needs to know that not all men see her that way. Some really do love her."

Emily and Jake shook hands and then Jake left. Emily got in her car and took something out of her purse that she had needed all day. It was something she hadn't needed in a long time. She pulled out a small bottle of Jack Daniel's Whisky and a bottle of pills. Emily had, had the items for a few days now and she had been staring at them in her office after her last few sessions with Lisa. She was tempted and she thought to herself that today was going to be the day she stepped back into the darkness. Emily turned on the car and drove to her next destination with the bottle of booze and pills lying next to her in the passenger seat.

∞ ∞ ∞ ∞ ∞

Emily arrived at her meeting. It was dark and cold outside, but it was a full moon and the moonlight was casting a shadow of light over the entrance of the building. Emily was going to an Alcoholics Anonymous meeting. She had not been in a long time because she felt like that she didn't need it anymore. Today she needed it. She went inside, got a cup of coffee, and took a seat. The meeting started and the person conducting it introduced himself.

"Hello, I'm Bill and I'm an alcoholic."

The crowd replied in unison. "Hello Bill."

Bill conducted them in the serenity prayer to start things off. The he asked the crowd if anybody would like to go first. Emily raised her hand. She walked up to the podium and said to the crowd.

"I'm Dr. Emily Bennett...I'm alcoholic and a drug addict."

The crowd replied in unison. "Hello Emily."

"I have been sober and drug free for three years, but today I almost took a drink and swallowed some pain killers. Today was the first day in three years that I really felt like I would do it again. I haven't needed these meetings in a long time, but today I did. Although I'm a doctor who helps mental patients today I needed help and that's why I'm here."

∞ ∞ ∞ ∞ ∞

While Emily was at her meeting Lisa was back in her room staring out of the window with bars on it into the cold dark night. The moonlight was casting a shadow over the parking lot and for the first time since she had been there she could see out beyond the parking lot and gated fence into the open fields behind the hospital. It was a bleak view because it looked like an untamed wilderness that would kill anybody that ventured into it. Rose was standing behind her. She said to Lisa.

"It's always better in here because we are protected by the bars. You'll see that in time."

"They say you're not real," Lisa replied. "They say I made you up."

"I'm as real as you want me to be."

"You seem real to me...can't deny that."

"You know what Lisa?"

"What's that Rose?"

"In this place, it's like you've always said – when in Rome do like the Romans do?"

It was starting to snow now and the snowflakes danced like floating spirits in the moonlight. Lisa wondered if the snow was real or was she imagining it. She replied to Rose.

"I think Rome is burning now."

"We can rebuild it. Just remember you made the right choice."

Lisa turned around and faced Rose. She replied. "Did I really make the right choice?"


~ The End ~

"Writing is a form of therapy;
sometimes I wonder how all those who do
not write, compose, or paint can manage to
escape the madness, melancholia, the panic
and fear which is inherent in a human
situation."

*~Graham Greene*

www.ingramcontent.com/pod-product-compliance
Lightning Source LLC
Chambersburg PA
CBHW050518190726
48284CB00003B/847